BLACKWOOD

Richard A. Powell II

Previous releases by Richard A. Powell II:

Neither Snow, Nor Rain, Nor Zombie Infection & Other Strange Tales
A Room Full of Keys
RejectGuy99
The Kill Series: *Kill Academy*, *Kill Team*, and *Kill Alone*

Available by order at bookstores and online worldwide.
www.richardapowellii.com

1

The Great Burn

Last year in the earliest days of August and an hour after the sun had risen, the small town of Blackwood, New Mexico awoke as it did on most weekdays. The coffee pots spat and gurgled to life, the local morning news blared on living room televisions, and the people rose to what they thought would be another typical day in their town. That day, however, turned out to be anything but typical, one that would forever alter each person's reality, some in ways they couldn't possibly have foreseen.

Few people in Blackwood witnessed the event that set the dusty, auburn landscape aflame. In the blink of an eye and moving east to west, the tremendous power and percussive force of a meteor flying through the air knocked down trees, telephone poles, old barns, dilapidated mobile homes, and many of the road signs in its path until it crashed just outside the town of Blackwood, New Mexico.

There have been many such incidents in human history. The vast majority cause little to no harm and leave no lasting effects on the population. There are, of course, exceptions. The Tunguska Event is the most well-known and biggest such event in recorded history.

In Siberia on the morning of June 30th, 1908, a massive 330-foot meteor flew over the Podkamennaya Tunguska River in Yeniseysk Governorate, now called Krasnoyarsk Krai, Russia. The meteor never even touched the ground, believed to have broken up before making impact. The effect, however, was nonetheless devastating.

The air burst of the meteor in flight killed only three people in the sparsely populated area of Siberia but leveled eighty million trees over more than three hundred square miles and registered an estimated 5.0 on the Richter scale. Had that event occurred in a highly populated area, it would have been catastrophic. And while the event in Blackwood was similar, the results and the consequences could not have been more different.

After flying over town, the Blackwood meteor did, in fact, hit the Earth, unlike the one from the Tunguska event. The impact shook the ground, cracking the dry, red soil in every direction, and further flattening any rickety structures that had not already been blown down by the incoming forces of the small meteor in flight. Animals in the wild and on local farms were not spared either. The seismic event took the legs out from under many horses and livestock, sending them crashing to the ground. One farmer witnessed one of his goats suddenly drop dead from no apparent trauma, while another flew off the ground and bounced just over his barb-wired enclosure, only to stumble and run away scared into a dense grove of trees that had somehow been spared the meteor's wrath. The farmer was never seen again, presumed dead.

The hole left in the earth was a perfect circle with the shoreline shallow and getting deeper as it went inward. A berm of soil a few feet high formed around the entire perimeter.

The explosion came next, sending flames, smoke, and debris across the flatlands of the mesa for three miles in all directions. From afar, the wall of hot air appeared at first to crawl, but with each passing second, it increased in speed exponentially. Those who laid eyes on the encroaching ground burst could not move away, staring helplessly into the advancing hell on Earth, like gazing into the most beautiful yet terrifying sunset.

For the people, the wind and gas came first, hot and stifling, stealing the breathable air. Oddly, no one suffocated. There wasn't time enough for that. The actual fire trailed too close behind and became their true reaper. Without mercy and without prejudice, hundreds of people were incinerated where they stood, lives deleted, buildings charred beyond all hope and left smoldering in ruin.

Many vehicles caught fire, and in short order, exploded, killing anyone inside. Buildings caught fire too, and some structures collapsed. The older brick buildings in town held up the best, although, their wooden roofs and windows were often blow off or burnt up.

Further from the epicenter, the chaos of the moment left some running in the streets, stumbling about as the ground shook, their bodies fully engulfed in flame, inevitably dropping them in random locations on the sidewalks, the yards, the parking lots. Many power lines drooped down as their poles bent over, with some lines snapping off completely, leaving their frayed ends sparking and dancing all over town.

One woman driving to work caught a view of the gas cloud in her rearview mirror and lost sight of the road, striking a mother and a child in a stroller, killing them both instantly. The driver attempted to swerve after the fact, hitting the curb and flipping her vehicle just as the firewall took hold of the street she was on.

The devastation left behind was nearly indescribable and as gut-wrenching a human catastrophe as had ever occurred in New Mexico. And as if the rogue meteor itself wasn't enough of a demonstration of the wrath of Mother Nature, twelve minutes after the fire took hold of Blackwood, sinister looking gray and black clouds rolled in from the northwest, bringing with them the most rainfall from a single system in recorded meteorological history. The crater formed by the impact quicky became a half-filled lake as the excess water streamed in to the hole at a staggering rate. The rain, as crazy as the timing was, actually served to keep the town from completely burning to the ground. The fires and remaining embers were washed out in short order, leaving behind an ashy, smoky landscape.

The entire event, later known as *The Great Burn*, happened in mere seconds. From that point forward, the identity of the town of Blackwood changed forever, a ghost of its former self, a sideshow for interstate travelers willing to veer off the highway for a two-hour excursion to bear witness to the charred wood left behind, the haunting landscape, and the lake formed by the impact crater.

For the people of Blackwood, time stood still, the trauma of *The Great Burn* too difficult for many to move past. The loss of life a tremendous burden, the survivor's guilt even more so.

On every corner, in every building, in every heart and soul, the reminders of that day lingered.

2

In Albuquerque...
About a year after *The Great Burn*

First thing in the morning on the average weekday, the hallways of the Overton Long-Term Care Facility in the north valley of Albuquerque, New Mexico bustled with foot traffic and chatter.

From room to room, the doctors and nurses and assistants handled their rounds with a rhythmic precision, the doctors especially. Pull the chart from the door. Read the notes. Enter the room. Brief conversation with the nurse. Stand at the end of the resident's bed. Speak briefly with said resident, if possible. Speak again to the nurse. Make a note on the chart. Leave the room. Onto the next.

The nurses and the assistants, of course, did most of the work. They handled the medications, answered the questions, changed the dressings and bedding and diapers, fed the meals, did the bathing, filled out most of the paperwork, on and on and on. Until witnessed and needed, we often underestimate the value of these people.

The resident in Room 45 heard none of the commotion, saw no one coming and going from his room. His meds were delivered via I.V., his food through a tube, his conversations only of an internal nature.

He had been at the facility for nearly seven months, comatose. Prior to that, the man had spent 5 months in the burn unit of the Grand Memorial Hospital across town. He was alive, he was breathing, and he had been badly burned over eighty percent of his body, to be precise. Beyond that, not much else was known of the man.

He had no hair on most of his body. None on his head or face, his arms or legs, his chest or back. The follicles had been replaced or blocked by scar tissue. The muscle structure on his face was so damaged that his eyes were permanently half-open and his lips shrunken to the point of exposing part of his gums and teeth. To the unaware and untrained, seeing the man was a ghastly and terrifying sight.

Whether or not he could feel the pain of his injuries, the skin grafting, and the recovery that followed was unknown. He was well-medicated to be sure, but that only goes so far. For all anyone knew, the man was constantly screaming from the depths of his own mind.

And in his mind, he wandered. There was no sense of time, no sense of space. His awareness of the waking world was reduced to soft whispers that sounded as if they were originating from long tunnels and brief flashes of light from the same.

His emotions and his memory are where he lived. A landscape of regret and pain and doubt. Granted, there were moments of peace and calm, but such is the human condition. We most often vividly remember our faults and our tears before recalling the success and the smiles. Being in a coma did not change that one iota. For him, the effect was often amplified.

After emerging from a long stretch of quiet and calm, the comatose man felt a breeze across his entire body. A hot wind. He could feel the fine particulates of the sand and dirt in the air as it pelted his face, the only truly exposed part of his body.

A small town appeared before him, a memory of one he once knew. He had been there thousands of times before, but something was different this time. He was present in a way he hadn't experienced before. Usually, he watched past events unfold or relived them, but that day, mixed in with the memories, there was an energy. It felt … alive.

Suddenly, that energy scared him. An immense force tugged on every fiber of his body and he began to convulse.

In the hospital room, the bed shook as the comatose man did. The readings on the monitor showed erratic spikes in heart rate and blood pressure. When the beeping of the alarm started, it rang loud and true, all the way down the hall.

3

Blackwood

The sign on the side of the road as one entered from the east read: Blackwood, Population 1665. The 1 had been covered by a black X and the five had been graffitied with white spray paint and replaced with a 6, malformed and dripping. Beneath that, also in white spray paint, were the words: Welcome to Hell. The front of the sign had otherwise remained unchanged for years; weathered, paint peeling, and now slightly askew from the blast of hot wind that passed during the event. The wood of the back of the sign, however, was charcoaled, and soot would still come off on a person's finger if they touched it. No one every bothered to replace the sign, perhaps as a warning to visitors, or maybe as a reminder to themselves about how much they lost, not that anyone really needed that.

The population total came from the last census and had surely dropped as a consequence of *The Great Burn*. For the hometown folks, a few would leave but most lived and died there, and new people rarely came around. That day, however, turned out to be different. Someone new had come to town, someone strange, someone...

Tall, dressed head to toe in black and shadowed in the face, the stranger stood on the sidewalk, staring down the road. An angry wind blew from behind him sending dirt, plastic bags, and all manner of debris down the street, yet his own wide-rimmed, black hat and ground-length black duster remained relatively still.

He took in the entire view before him like the master of his domain, studying, observing. Blackwood, however, was not his town, and he certainly not the master of it. How he had come to be in that particularly place, in that particular time, and for what particular purpose was unknown. One minute, the dusty and nearly deserted road was empty, and the next minute it was not. That was all anyone could say.

"Wind picking up again. Might have another freakin' dust storm moving in," Phil, the local mechanic and town drunk announced to anyone listening as he returned from the bathroom. He took his seat in the booth closest to the front door at The Empty Diner. He always faced the door so he could watch people come and go as he sipped his coffee and ate his breakfast, the only decent meal he ever managed to get in. Once the work day began and the last drops of his coffee fell, his only intake for the rest of the day would be beer or whiskey. Meaningful conversations after 5 pm were all but a lost art for Phil, aside from, of course, the imaginary ones he held with the booze demons that haunted him.

The diner, though, was a cheery place where all the townsfolk gathered to gossip, to eat, and to complain about this or that. With no tavern in town, the diner had to serve all those purposes. The sign outside read: Where the seats may be empty but the cups are always full. Home of the bottomless $1.00 cup of coffee.

It was the only such place in the small, desert town of Blackwood, but the words regarding the seats being empty were mostly untrue. There were always patrons around, most arriving like clockwork for their favorite sandwich or a simple cup of joe.

"Great. Another damn mess to clean up," Ted barked as he scraped the flat-top grill from behind the giant pass-through where he placed the orders as they were plated.

"You live on the damn mesa, you live with the damn dust, Ted," said Raelle, the only employee who had worked at The Empty Diner for as long as Ted, and the only one who could get away with such sass. "Don't like it, move to the Midwest. We'll clean it up, just like last time, just like every time."

Normally, Ted would have given the sass right back but after he turned from the grill, popped his head up, and glanced out the front door, he jumped back a little, startled by the sudden presence of a strange character across the street, a man dressed all in black.

The man stood on the sidewalk on the opposite side of the road, staring down the street. With a shadow over the man's face, his exact focus remained a mystery.

"Where the hell did you come from?" Ted kept his glare on the stranger, not once backing down. The stranger did not move either. Not many people came to their remote desert town, a little off the beaten path as it was. Ted was sure people came through all the time, but for the life of him, he couldn't remember specifically the last time he saw a stranger. Might have been a week, might have been a month. Ted began wondering if dementia had started to take hold.

"Who are you talking to?" Raelle asked Ted as she wiped the counter with a bleached washcloth, her long, slender frame allowing her to reach all the way past the counters edge with her heels barely off the ground.

"Who's the weirdo across the street?" Phil chimed in with scrambled eggs in his mouth. He swallowed his mouthful and took a sip of coffee, but his eyes stayed on the stranger.

Raelle looked up and caught sight of the man too. They were all mesmerized. The man was ... odd. That was the word that entered all of their minds in that moment.

On August 5th and already nearing one hundred degrees outside at just 8:21 a.m., anyone covered head to toe in black wouldn't last long, but that was only part of the problem. There was something eerie, even menacing about how he stood there motionless, watching. Other than the occasional dust storm, the weather in town was nearly always sunny, hot, and still. That day, the calm disappeared and was replaced with a gradually graying sky and ill-winds that followed the presence of the stranger. No one seemed to notice the coincidence.

Their eyes remained fixated on the stranger. As if he could feel their gaze on him, the man slowly and deliberately turned his head toward the diner, and about halfway to a full 90-degree turn, his head suddenly snapped into a position facing them head on. Each one of their hearts skipped a beat, their nerves unraveling faster and faster with each breath.

"I ... I," Ted mumbled, but before he could squeak out another word, his upper lip tingled with moisture. With eyes still locked on the stranger, Ted put a finger to his mustache area, then brought the finger into view. His nose had started bleeding, something that hadn't happened to him since before *The Great Burn*. He tried to turn away from the door to go grab some tissue from the bathroom but found himself unable to. A single drop of blood fell from his upper lip, splatting onto his stainless-steel prep counter.

From nowhere, a stiff gust of wind blew hard against the front of the diner, grains of sand aggressively dancing across the glass. The foundation and the roof creaked in resistance, and the windows rattled just short of shattering. All three inside the diner remained still, only their eyes briefly closing in reaction. An unknown force held their catatonic state and would simply not let go. As they opened their eyes, they noticed the skies outside clearing, the wind slowing to a breeze, and no trace of the man in black.

Ted's nosebleed had been flowing harder with each passing second, but suddenly stopped with the disappearance of the stranger. And he could move again, he discovered by successfully rising to his tiptoes to get a better view through the kitchen opening. They often joked about how he and Raelle looked like the number ten when they stood next to each other, although, Ted's version of the zero was five inches shorter than her number one, and about forty pounds shy of the perfect rotund. He made a point to remind everyone of that each time the topic arose.

He suddenly remembered the blood on his face. Ted grabbed a nearby towel, moistened it in the hand-washing sink, which was to the right of the swinging kitchen door, and cleaned up the blood. He scrubbed extra hard on his upper lip to get the quickly crusting red from his mustache. Looking in the small mirror above the sink and turning his head left and right to get a better view, he was happy enough to drop the rag in the sink and return to his station. When he got there, he couldn't help but stare out of the window and get lost in his thoughts.

Phil knew his blood pressure had dropped because the ringing in his ears had grown louder. The sensation of his head swelling with pressure gave him an instant migraine, not so different from those times when he hadn't had a drink in over six hours. When his wife was killed in a car accident some years back, his social drinking flourished into full-blown weekend benders, and later when the four children she left him with all perished in *The Great Burn*, every night was a good night for getting blasted. The second he punched the clock after closing up his auto mechanic's shop at the end of each day meant a steady stream of beer flowed until he grew too tired for the slow buzz, finishing off his evening with swigs of Wild Turkey whiskey. He often passed out right in his favorite living room recliner only to be awoken the next morning by his only shop employee Toby pounding on the front screen door.

Unlike Ted, Phil's physical reactions did not cease after the man disappeared. His headache, in fact, grew worse to the point where he felt the need to vomit, and he did. He turned his head away from the window just in time to hurl his breakfast and coffee right onto the table in front of him. Out of disgust, he slipped out of the booth and onto his feet, using the edge of the table to keep his balance, surprised to discover his legs were wobbly.

As Ted and Phil had their unusual experiences, a bizarre nervousness overcame Raelle, and along with it a trembling in her fingers. Without warning, she was unable to catch her breath. She put her left hand to her throat as she gasped for air. When it finally stopped, she bent over and took in as much air as she could, as quickly as she could. From the back of her throat came a bunch of water-like fluid that she spit onto the floor. No one else saw it. She grabbed a washcloth from under the counter and cleaned up the water, tossing it in the laundry bin when she finished. Rising up, she saw that

Phil had thrown up, so she took two fresh washcloths, wetting one in the sink, and rushed over to Phil.

"Oh, Phil, are you alright?" Raelle dabbed his mouth with one of the rags. Looking at his face, she grew even more concerned at how pale he had become. "Horey, you need to go see Sean. You look like a ghost. And that reminds me. Where is Sean? He didn't come in for his coffee this morning."

Speaking through the service window, Ted said, "Who knows. Probably went straight into the office today."

"Maybe," Raelle replied.

Dr. Sean Atwater was the only doctor in their small town and he frequently stopped in to grab two coffees and two pastries for himself and his office manager. That morning, he failed to make an appearance.

Phil staggered a little but kept his balance.

Raelle pulled a chair from a nearby table and shoved it right behind Phil. "You need to sit." She grabbed his arm and guided him back. He resisted.

"I'm ok. And I don't need to go see the doctor. I'll be fine."

After deciding his nose was no longer going to be a problem, Ted left the kitchen to get a look at Phil. He shared Raelle's analysis. "Phil, you need to go see the doc. You look like someone just stole ten years from your life."

With little strength left to stay on his feet, Phil finally slumped down to the chair, rubbed his forehead to ease the headache, all the while squinting at the light coming through the windows. The brightness made his head feel worse.

"You're going. I'll drive you over there." Raelle left no room for argument." She hustled over to the counter and grabbed a glass of ice water, handing it to Phil. He took a few sips to clear the vomit and stomach acid from his mouth which was beginning to burn. The sour taste remained.

With heavy breaths between every few words, Phil said, "Alright. I'll go. Jesus. But before we do, is anybody ... going to say anything ... about what just happened? What ... the fuck ... was that?"

With no eye contact to either, Ted shrugged his shoulders, not really wanting to discuss it. For reasons he could not explain, the presence of the stranger and the wind storm brought about memories of his brother Frank, sister-in-law Regina, his niece Messiah, and nephew, Isaiah, all killed in *The Great Burn*. They were a close-knit family, and with no other relatives in Blackwood or anywhere else, the loss was unequivocal.

He couldn't recall finding their badly charred bodies or filing any official reports with the police or medical professionals, or afterwards, any funeral services. Perhaps the shock helped to bury those memories deep down where he could never find them. Perhaps it was just too difficult to endure the thoughts, and even at that moment, his psyche would not allow his mind to travel there.

"I'm more concerned about you right now, Phil. Can you get on your feet?" Raelle urged. She grabbed his right arm at the elbow and guided him up.

"I think I can walk down there. He put eyes on the vomit he left on his table. "Sorry about the mess."

"I'll pull my car around. And don't worry about the damn mess." She hollered, "Ted!"

He did not respond, his eyes fixed on the front windows and his view across the street. An impression of the man in black had been burned into his mind's eye, like a ghostly image in the corner of an old black and white photo, unnoticeable until pointed out by someone.

"Ted!" Raelle barked as she snapped her fingers four times as loud as she could.

Ted emerged from his trance and finally spoke. "The storm stopped." Ted said, monotone, listless. The sun shone again and the wind had all but disappeared. A plastic fountain soda cup without a lid had settled on the sidewalk between the road and front door to the restaurant. The street had become eerily calm. Normally at that hour, there was at least some activity.

"Ted, can you please keep an eye on Phil while I bring my car around. I realize some weird shit just happened but you need to pull yourself together so I can get him to see the doctor before he strokes out or something."

Ted decided to stay mum on the nosebleed. "Yeah, yeah. I got it." Ted broke his eyes from the road. "You'll be ok, bud. I'm sure it's nothing."

Raelle swung around and jogged to the break room at the back of the kitchen to grab her purse. She returned with her keys in hand. "I'll be right back." She didn't wait for a response. She flew out of the front door and headed left down the sidewalk to the small parking lot on the side of the two-story brick building.

Her 2007, four-door, maroon Chevrolet Malibu sat at the far end of the parking lot, closest to the small wooden enclosure that housed the restaurant's gray grease bin, blue recycle dumpster, and brown garbage dumpster. The only other vehicles occupying the fourteen spaces were two pickup trucks.

The Malibu flew out of its original spot and down the street before screeching to a halt in the lone handicapped parking spot directly in front of the entrance of The Empty Diner. Out popped Raelle, leaving the car door open. She ran back in. The bell above the door rang out.

"I'm feeling much better now," Phil said.

"You're going." Raelle looked to Ted. "Help me get him to the car please."

They each cradled one of Phil's arms and guided him outside and into the car. He walked mostly under his own strength. They ended up just being there in case he lost his balance, but it turned out he didn't need assistance.

Once inside the car and just before Raelle could shut her door, Ted spoke up. "I'll get everything cleaned up while you're gone."

"Ok. I won't be long."

"Hey, you notice there's no one on the street, and no one else has come into the diner?" Ted asked. "Strange, right?"

"I guess so. We'll sort it out when I get back," Raelle said just before she closed the door.

Ted stood motionless as he watched them drive away. A series of images popped into his head, ones his mind created because he wasn't there to actually witness the deaths of his family.

He closed his eyes and imagined he was standing on the street facing his brother's house. The family was on the porch, his brother Frank, wife Regina, their daughter Messiah, and their son Isaiah. They stood all in a row, statuesque, like mannequins in a department store window. Ted's eyes could not be diverted from little Isaiah's face, the odd caricature of it, haunting in its doll-like appearance. And yet the eyes. The eyes were very much like his own.

From nowhere, an intense heat built up, and without time to react, flames engulfed everything within his view. He lost his breath. The house crumbled into ash and his family melted like plastic, their bodies pooling in a mocha-colored goo right on top of the blackened remains of the house. He reached out, mouth agape, no sound escaping.

Ted opened his eyes and gasped for air, a single tear falling down the left side of his face. He was not a man who cried. He had yet to do so at the loss of his family until that moment. Something had changed. Ted knew it. He could feel it. A fear of unknown origins had settled in.

Back inside The Empty Diner, Ted started cleaning up Phil's mess, still a bit shaken himself by the morning's oddities. He tried desperately to push away the images from his head by thinking about anything else. It failed. With no one in the diner to serve or help take his mind off them, the thoughts continued to swirl. He debated on whether he should just close up and go home, the idea of a stiff drink and his warm bed an overpowering temptation.

He nearly jumped out of his skin at the screech of the bathroom door swinging open. Ted's eyes darted to the right. From the shadows emerged Toby McNamee, a tall, brute of a man of Scotch-Irish decent, and he wore it physically: freckled, carrot red short hair that was just long enough to start curling, and deep, ocean blue eyes. He was built more like a linebacker than an auto mechanic, and it came naturally. The one word that popped into everyone's mind when they first came across Toby was big. He was just ... big.

"Jesus, Toby, you scared the holy shit outta me."

A confused look drew across Toby's face as he walked over to Ted. He looked around, finding it strange there was no one else in the diner. "Where's Phil?"

Ted finished wiping the table and let out a sigh. "I forgot you were even in there. Some seriously weird shit just went down."

Past history speaking, Toby instantly assumed Phil had done something stupid but just as quickly dismissed it knowing Phil wouldn't have been drinking that early in the day.

"What happened?" At the table, Toby saw their breakfast plates and glasses had been removed. "You okay, Ted? Your eyes are all red."

"Oh ... no, I'm fine. Raelle took Phil to see Sean. He threw up all over the table and got kinda pale. She insisted on running him over there."

"Damn. Really? I better get over there then."

"I think he was fine," Ted defended. "But you wouldn't believe." Ted started talking really fast as he knew Toby was on his way out of the door. "The wind started blowing and the skies turned dark and this weird fuckin' guy showed up across the street, dressed all in black like an outlaw cowboy or some shit. Then my nose started bleeding and Phil got sick, and then all of a sudden, the guy was gone. Gone. Poof."

Toby heard every word but didn't really process it. "You can tell me all about it later," he said as he left the diner. His truck was parked in the front of the building in the third space down to his right. He ran as he pulled the keys from his pocket, worried about his boss.

If Phil Reece had a real friend, it was Toby. They had been working together at Phil's automotive repair shop, Reece Automotive, since it opened ten years prior. Phil and his wife Hanna had just moved to Blackwood with their 2-year-old twin boys, Oscar and Oliver, to help Hanna's ailing mother in her final days. Three months later, they inherited the house and some cash, enough for Phil to purchase the old repair shop that had been closed for five years.

As Phil drove to the shop one morning to continue prepping the place for business, he spotted the then seventeen-year-old Toby leaning over the engine of his truck, presumably making a repair of some sort. Phil knew he wouldn't be able to run the shop alone, and in a small town, the pickings would be slim for employees. He took a chance and stopped to talk to the kid.

Sure enough, Toby knew his way around cars, mostly out of necessity. And without anything else better to do since he dropped out of high school that year, Toby accepted the job offer and the rest was history. From that day forward, Toby became Phil's right-hand man. And when the drinking became an issue for Phil after Hanna was killed, ironically enough, in an automobile accident while traveling to Albuquerque, Toby became Phil's ride to and from work, and to their morning stop at the diner for breakfast beforehand.

In the year prior to *The Great Burn*, the town tolerated, reservedly, Phil's drinking and the behavior that sometimes accompanied it. Everyone knew how hard it would be for Phil to raise his children alone, so out of guilt and passiveness, Phil was left mostly to his own devices. The car accident was two years, one month, and eighteen days before the fire. In the ten years of living in Blackwood, they managed to have two more children, May Sierra Reece and Katelyn Dinah Reece, affectionately known as Maysi and Kadi. At the time of their mother's death, they were ages seven and five, respectively. Their older twin brothers were just short of ten years old then.

When the children needed something, they counted on their teachers, their neighbors, and of course, Toby. He became a surrogate parent of sorts, but often reminded the kids who their real father was and how hard life had been for him. "I know he's not perfect but he does the best he can," Toby would say.

After Hanna's death, Phil drank but functioned. He could be approached and would interact, but at times he was distant and aloof. When fire engulfed the town of Blackwood and his children taken by flame, there was a clear metamorphosis. He was hungover and lying in a ditch about two miles from town when the event happened, and thusly did not bear witness to the horror of his four children being burned alive, but he could not keep his mind from creating an image in his head. From that point on, at least after business hours and on the weekends, he became more like the neighbor's snarling dog that everyone went out of their way to avoid by walking on the other side of the street. On an August Saturday morning, Phil went from a distressed and beleaguered widow to the town drunk, and there would be no going back.

4

The only doctor's office in town sat on the corner of Main Street and Cooley Avenue. The newly renovated, single story structure looked out of place sitting at the end of a long row of connected and aging two, three, and four-story brick buildings. The landscaping was fresh and new, mostly river rock and various orange, yellow, and green perennials and bushes. The office represented a change in times, a changing of the guard.

Dr. Sean Atwater inherited the building from his dear friend and mentor, Dr. Harold Mayweather, Blackwood's longtime and once sole physician, a man who had still made house calls when needed and had done his job until the day he died of a heart attack at age eighty-six.

Sean spent his entire childhood in Blackwood and often longed to get away, his ambitions and intelligence greater than any small desert town could ever satisfy. With a perfect

G.P.A. and an SAT score in the high 1400s, Sean positioned himself to leave Blackwood forever, and Dr. Mayweather encouraged him at every opportunity.

After attending Stanford for his undergraduate degree, Sean flew to the opposite coast for medical school at Columbia in New York. He fell in love with New York and with a woman, Vera, who to a small-town westerner like Sean, was cultured and exotic and charming. Her tall, slender frame and short bobbed espresso brown hair attracted him instantly, who as a runner, understood the practicality of her hair style. He could have only hoped she shared his love of fitness and he was not disappointed. One of their first dates was jogging through Central Park as the foliage turned every shade of orange, yellow, and red. They joked later about how it was almost too perfect, like some heavily scripted moment from a romantic comedy. In short order, Sean could no longer envision a happy life with anyone else or in any other place.

Going back to his hometown in New Mexico to live again never occurred to him, but when the call came in from Janice Mayweather that her husband had passed, a process was set in motion that would lead him back.

With Phil hanging on her arm, Raelle frantically pushed open the metal-framed door to Dr. Atwater's office lobby. There were no other patients in the brightly lit waiting room. As always, Nurse and Office Manager Talia Simmons sat behind the receptionist wall, busy typing on the computer. Thursday was typically the slowest day as most patients preferred appointments on Monday or Friday, so even though they had been open since 8 a.m., the first scheduled appointment was often not until after 9 a.m.

"Hey, Talia. Phil here got sick at the diner. Think Sean can see him, just to make sure he's okay?" Raelle made no mention of her own physical reaction.

"Goodness. What happened?" Talia popped from her seat and came through the door just to Raelle's left.

"Long story short, he threw up all over his table and got really pale, could barely stay on his feet."

Talia grabbed Phil's arm and put two fingers on his wrist to check his pulse. She counted in her head while looking at her watch. "Pulse seems fine. Let's sit down here and I'll go get Sean." Together, the ladies lowered Phil into the closest seat.

"I'm really feeling much better now," Phil said. "This ain't necessary."

"Well, as you can see," answered Talia, "we aren't exactly full-up right now. I'll feel much better if you let the doctor just take a quick peek at you," Talia's voice was sweet and comforting.

Phil nodded.

"Hang on one minute." Talia put up an index finger and disappeared into the back area.

Less than a minute later, Talia emerged. "Come on back, Phil. Can you walk by yourself?"

"Of course." On his own power but with Raelle close by, Phil rose to his feet and slowly walked through the door and into exam room number one, the first door on his left.

Talia followed. Once in the room and with Phil seated on a black vinyl chair near the window, Raelle felt confident enough to head back to work.

"Shit," Raelle said. "I just realized Toby was in the bathroom at the diner. I'm going to send him over when I get back. Okay, Phil?"

"Thanks, hun."

"Small town, bub. We gotta look out for each other." She gave him a big wink. "We'll see you tomorrow."

They waved to each other and off she went.

In the parking lot, Raelle saw Toby's truck barreling down the road. She waited outside her car to talk to him.

Toby shot into the spot next to her and exited the vehicle with equal urgency.

"Hey. What the heck happened? Is he okay?"

"I think he'll be fine. Sean is gonna check him out. I take it you talked to Ted?"

"Yep."

"So, how are you feeling?"

"Me?" Toby pointed to his own chest. "Why? I'm fine."

"Oh. Well. Something ... strange happened. I don't know." Raelle used her left hand to rub the side of her face as she pondered how to describe the event. She shook her head with nothing more to add that wouldn't make her sound insane.

"Are you sure *you're* okay? Ted looked like he'd had better mornings, that's for sure."

"I think so. It's Phil I'm worried about."

"I'm going in then. I'll swing by later and let you know how he is."

"Sounds good. Thanks."

"Sean'll be just a sec," Talia said.

Phil smiled and nodded.

Talia left the room, leaving the door open behind her. From her seat at the front desk, she could keep an eye on Phil until Sean went in. She sat back down in her leather office chair and picked up right where she left off on the task she'd been working on. Every ten seconds or so, she glanced over to exam room one.

Phil sat quietly, looking around the room. He had been there a few times before with his kids but never as a patient. He avoided doctors whenever possible. He got tired of hearing the same old shit: you need to lose weight, you need to stop drinking, your blood pressure is too high. He understood the problems he had, he just didn't care or have the will to do anything about them.

Dr. Sean Atwater entered the exam room with no eye contact, shutting the door and stopping to wash his hands before approaching Phil. He felt out of sorts that day. Had his normal morning routine not been disrupted by him sleeping through his alarm and being late to the office, he might very well have been at The Empty Diner when the odd man arrived.

He had awoken from a restless, disturbing sleep, something he had grown quite accustomed to. When he slept, he was sent to another world where his loss and anguish surrounded him like a thick fog set out over a vast mesa. There were no boundaries and no end.

While awake, time had little meaning to him anymore. Each day held a routine. He'd rise, shower and dress, stop off at the local diner for a cup of coffee and a pastry, go to the office, go home, go to bed. There were seemingly no other events in between, at least none he could recall.

Life had become a series of minor blips on a radar screen that no one paid any attention to. He wasn't alone in the drifting. The entire town of Blackwood operated on much the same pattern. Mass tragedy often does that, but for some people, the after effects were much worse than others, and many of them were finding it hard to let go.

That morning, unbeknownst to Sean, his alarm had been blaring for nearly twenty-five minutes. When he finally opened his eyes and discovered the actual time, he sprung from bed and got dressed, skipping his usual shave and shower, and left the house heading straight for the office. His routine pitstop for coffee would need to wait until he could check his morning appointments.

On the drive to work, what little of his dreams he could remember sat heavy in his mind. There was always a voice, one he recognized, one he frantically searched for. Another night of fear, another day of desperately wanting to forget. The nightmares had gotten worse in previous weeks, which he lent to the upcoming anniversary of *The Great Burn*. It was going to be a rough couple of weeks. Everyone knew it. Most of all Dr. Atwater.

For Sean, mental distraction was the order of the day. He remained professional, however, turning to face Phil with a casual smile and nod, the best he could do in that moment in the role of comforting hometown doctor.

"Talia says you got sick at the diner a bit ago. How you feeling now?" As they spoke, Sean took Phil's blood pressure.

"Doing much better. Strangest thing. Sitting eatin' breakfast. Kinda bizarre storm rolled through, real cloudy and windy but no rain, and then we see this guy across the street. Wore all black, long coat, hat, crazy getup in this heat."

"Blood pressure's a little high. Could be the booze there." Sean didn't admonish, only stated it as fact. Sean knew Phil and Phil knew Sean. The doctor didn't mince words and Phil couldn't deny the truth. "Lift up your shirt."

"So, we're all looking at this weirdo across the street and suddenly I can't move, like I have no control over my body."

Sean's ears perked up at the notion of Phil losing mobility. Stroke or seizure were the first conditions he thought of.

"Hang on there. You said you couldn't move? Like ... an arm or a leg?"

"No, like nothing. My whole body. Frozen. You know, like cata ... chronic."

"You mean catatonic."

"Whatever."

"Sounds like you may have had a seizure."

"Don't you have to be jerking and flopping around and shit when you have a seizure? I was frozen."

"Not necessarily. It's called an absence seizure, but it seems you were aware the whole time, and well, that's an anomaly."

"And, I didn't tell Raelle or Ted this, but I smelled something funny while I was frozen, kind of like a campfire."

"Campfire, huh?" Sean's mind instantly went back to the day of *The Great Burn* but he wiped it from his mind as quickly as it had entered. "Well that certainly sounds like a seizure. And not to beat a dead horse, but extreme alcohol use has been known to cause seizures." Sean removed the stethoscope from Phil's chest. "Heartbeat seems regular, no murmurs, nothing erratic. You can put your shirt back down." Phil did. "Turn your head to the left for me." He pulled an otoscope from a drawer just to his right and put it to Phil's right ear.

"That guy across the road, I'm telling ya, when we all looked at him, it was just ... weird."

"Go ahead and turn the other way."

"Absolute craziest shit I've ever seen, and I've seen a lot."

"I don't know, Phil. Hard for me to understand since I wasn't there. All I can do is examine you right now, so let's just deal with what we have in front of us." He placed the otoscope on the counter above the drawer he had pulled it from and turned back to face Phil. "I'm going to refer you to a guy in Albuquerque. You're going to need more testing, a proper EEG, blood work."

"Oh shit, man. I don't wanna go through all that. Can't you just give me a scrip that'll fix me up?"

"No. We don't even know a hundred percent what's wrong with you. My medical opinion is that you need to go see a neurologist right away. In fact, I'll have Talia make a call and see if we can find you an opening in the next couple of days."

Sean walked to the door and opened it. "Talia, can you call Dr. Augenbach at St. Joseph's and see if we can get Phil in to see him in the next few days?"

She spun her chair around to face Sean. "What are we looking at?"

"Possible seizure, need EEG, bloodwork, the whole gamut. Tell him I need a favor for a friend."

"Will do. Tell Phil that Toby is out here to take him home. Talia whipped back around to finish what she was doing.

"You hear that?" Sean asked after turning back to Phil.

"Yep."

"Phil, I want you to take it easy for the next few days, no work, at least until after you see Dr. Augenbach. If you have any symptoms at all, even the slightest thing, you call 9-1-1."

"No sweat. Toby'll be around. Slow at the shop right now anyways." Phil shrugged his shoulders. "So, is that it?"

"I'm also going to tell you to lay off the drink for a few days too."

Phil made a face that made it pretty clear he was going to struggle with that request or just flat out ignore it.

Sean put his hands up in retreat. "Wouldn't be doing my job if I didn't at least say it. That's it then. If you have any questions, just call the office."

Phil got to his feet much easier this time, walking past Sean with relative ease.

As Phil walked through the doorway, Sean said, "Have a good rest of the week."

"Yep. You too."

In the lobby, Phil was greeted by Toby and a look of concern he had never seen on his friend's face.

"I'm okay. Feeling a million times better now."

"What the hell happened?"

"Hang on a sec," Phil said, putting up his index finger before turning to the service window. "Hey, Talia. Anything you need from me?"

"Nope. I'll call you with the appointment information later today."

"Great. Thanks." Phil faced Toby again.

"Just take me home. I'm tired. Doc says I can't work for a few days. We can talk about it later. Gonna make me go to another doctor up north and get more tests. I don't know if I'll even go. Bit of an overreaction if you ask me."

"Well, try not to worry about that right now. You look a little pale, but otherwise, no worse than usual." Toby sighed in relief.

Not that he demonstrated it well, but Phil was the closest thing Toby had to a father figure. Toby's own father had left his mother when Toby was just three years old and they never saw him again. Phil gave Toby his first job, the only one he had ever had. Phil's own kids became his de facto siblings, and later, Toby felt more like a surrogate parent when the drinking escalated. Before *The Great Burn*, Toby had dinner at the Reece house almost every day. Phil was far more than a boss and a friend to Toby. They had become family.

They left the office together, each with different forms of anxiety centering around completely different things.

Toby worried for the health of his boss. He often thought of Phil as a ticking time bomb. He knew that one day the timer would strike double zeroes and that would be it. He had been mentally preparing for the possibility of Phil dying for years, but after *The Great Burn*, he understood the timer had accelerated.

Remembering the morning's events at the diner, Phil's angst fell to the entire town of Blackwood, though he couldn't quite grab hold of why. It was just a feeling in the pit of his stomach. The stranger from the street disrupted more than just Phil's body. In some unknown capacity, Phil understood the stranger's presence would have more of an effect on the town then anyone understood, like a building on fire with one smoldering room devoid of air just waiting for somebody to open the door.

Boom! Backdraft.

5

The area before Sean was gray and thick with smoke. It reeked with the all too familiar smell of burnt wood. Soft voices murmured but none could be distinguished. Through the miasma came figures, a crowd, too many people in such a small space. They moved to and from as the gray moved, fluid and amoebic, almost in slow motion.

Sean stood confused by the environment and his place in it. His heart raced. The atmosphere held a general sense of dread and anxiety. The people brushed up against him, ethereal, faceless ghosts passing him by. He waded through the sea, moving much like the rest until he heard someone that he recognized call out to him.

"Daddy," said the distant voice, muddled like it was spoken into a cupped hand. "Daddy."

Suddenly panicked, Sean looked around but nothing unusual drew his attention. He turned his head to focus his ear and waited.

"Daddy?"

Sean snapped his head around.

"Where are you?" the voice asked.

He turned his head a few inches to his left, listening intently. "That voice. I ... know it. I know it. Gabe? Gabriel!"

"Find me. You're lost, Daddy."

"I'm lost? I can't see you. Where are you?"

Sean walked in the direction he believed the voice had originated but he couldn't be certain. There was too much interference in his mind, and in that unfamiliar place full of fog, Sean felt completely disoriented. There were too many others as well, blocking his path and hindering his movement. As he sidestepped through the crowd, he felt like he was making no progress.

"I'm here, Daddy."

As he shuffled, he caught glimpses of the empty faces, if they could be called faces, and they startled him. Confusion and fear grabbed him. His steps became heavy. The space around him closed in. He reached in agony toward the voice, fighting the others for space.

"I can't find you, Gabe," Sean called out. "I can't see you."

"Sean!" A voice called out, but not that of Gabe.

The others swarmed Sean, pushing him back even as he fought. He lost all momentum, sliding back and back, faster and faster.

"Sean!" The voice came louder that time. "Dr. Atwater!"

Suddenly, the crowd released him and he fell, slow for a moment but suddenly at light speed until...

Sean opened his eyes and jerked his head from the office desk.

"Dr. Atwater? Are you ok?" Talia asked with growing concern. That was the fourth time in as many weeks that she found him asleep at this desk. "I've been yelling and yelling at you. I just about came over and smacked the back of your head."

"Yes, Talia. I'm fine. Thank you. What time is it?" He never wore a watch anymore and there was no clock in his office. For him, and for Blackwood, it seemed like time stood still.

"Closing time."

Sean sat confused. *How the hell is it the end of the day already?* He remembered seeing Phil in the morning but could recall nothing after that.

Sean rubbed his forehead and ran his fingers through is bristly, short-cropped hair. It had been a rich brown just a few years ago, but since moving back to Blackwood, it had steadily peppered itself with gray. Even at thirty-nine years old and the undue stress of that past year, the change was too early for his liking.

"You've been doing this a lot lately. Maybe it's time to go see someone. So, where does a doctor go when he needs to see a doctor, Doctor?" She smiled but her question was serious.

"Albuquerque, that's where. And don't worry about it. I really am fine. Just a little insomnia."

"Can I give you a dollar's worth of free advice?" Talia asked with one hand on the door knob, the other on her hip.

"Are you really asking?" He rose from his chair, closed the manila folder on the desk in front of him, and turned to face her.

"It's been a year, Sean. It was terrible for all of us, especially those with kids."

With Gabe still on his mind and the lingering sensation of being lost without him, Sean started to tune Talia out.

"Maybe the kind of doctor you need is not of the medical variety." When she said the words, she meant them for Sean but also for herself.

Sean didn't care much for that particular line of questioning or the suggestion, although, somewhere inside, he knew she was right. Everyone in town lost someone: family, friends, neighbors. The town was small enough that everyone knew everyone else, so even though the losses were hardest in the microcosm, they too were felt wholly by the community at large.

"You lost someone too and you're not exactly the poster child for perfect mental health either." Sean immediately regretted the tone but he couldn't stop. "Not without Jorge and that whole mess." He knew he had crossed a line with the last part and desperately wanted to fold the words back into his mouth but it was too late for that.

For years, Talia held a terrible secret from her husband, Jorge, and from everyone. She loved her husband beyond words but there was one area of their relationship where they were diametrically opposed. Jorge came from a large family with seven siblings and he had always imagined himself married with an equally large brood. Talia, on the other hand, had no siblings and had no desire to have children of her own. She played neutral on the topic over the years, but in truth, she was firm on her desires.

When she became pregnant, she secretly terminated the pregnancy, and when it happened again two years later, she did it again. It was then she realized she could no longer risk her health, her emotional state, and most importantly, for Jorge to discover the truth. Her third and final deception came when she had her tubes tied without Jorge's knowledge.

Other than the medical staff that performed the procedures, Sean was the only other person on the planet that knew Talia's secret. During a particularly tough time in Talia and Jorge's relationship, she needed a shoulder to cry on and Sean took on that responsibility.

In the years since she shared her story with him, Sean had never once thought of mentioning it to her again, but that day, with his mood in a dark place and his mind on his family, he let it slip. Under normal circumstances, the incident was way beyond his character and personality.

Talia's face remained stoic. "Go home ... Doctor." Disgusted, she pushed the door away from her body, leaving the office to go home herself. She had heard enough.

Sean took a deep breath and a step toward the doorway. "Talia!" He sighed and scratched his head. "Sorry, that was over..." Sean stopped mid-sentence upon hearing the sound of the front door bell. She was out of the building. The damage had been done.

"Damn it!" He flopped back down into his chair, the base creaking from the sudden weight change. He had been needing to buy a new desk chair for years. He just couldn't see fit to replace the one he inherited from his mentor, Dr. Mayweather. It was the one remnant left from before Sean took over.

When he stepped through the doors of the office for the first time after returning to Blackwood, Sean knew right away there would need to be a significant remodel. The décor, the furniture, the filing system, even the exterior and landscaping, had not been updated in twenty years. Taking the reins of a small-town family practitioner was the perfect excuse to modernize the place, but when he stepped into Harold's office and saw the old, cracking burgundy leather desk chair, it spoke to him.

The foam behind the well-worn leather cushioning was barely holding up and the wheels and the base squeaked, but when he sat down to give it a try, he somehow felt the responsibility of keeping Blackwood alive passing to him. Perhaps it was from the spirit of Dr. Mayweather or maybe from the town itself. He didn't believe in ghosts. The idea defied reason or explanation, but he knew what he sensed that day.

6

Talia shuffled out of the door, purse in hand, her neatly French-braided long ponytail swaying behind her as she walked to her car. At just under five and half feet tall and a little stocky, she could move faster than her body would suggest.

She came from a long line of medical professionals. Her parents, in fact, met while working together. Her father, Lyle Simmons, worked as an anesthesiologist at the same hospital in Denver, Colorado as her mother, Rosa Guzman, did as an RN. For three years they would pass each other in the halls, smile, flirt a little, until finally one day, Rosa grew tired of wondering if Lyle would ever ask her out, so she took charge of the situation. The workplace and hallway chemistry they often felt turned out to be real, and within six months they were married. A year later, Talia was born.

Once in her car, Talia threw her purse on the passenger seat, started the car, put her hands the wheel, and just paused. Sean left her enraged. She thought about his words and wondered if she were truly mad at him or if there was some truth behind what he had said. She was too angry to care. Yes, Talia suffered like everyone else in town. She functioned well during the day, did her job, and always kept her mood in check, but at home, alone, the absence of her husband Jorge and the memories of her past haunted her relentlessly.

Gripping the steering wheel tightly, she swung between wanting to cry and wanting to scream. She managed to keep from doing either one. She tried to calm her nerves with internal dialogue.

I don't really need this right now. Like I'm not stressed out enough.

She closed her eyes for a moment.

Oh, Jesus, Talia. Just try to breathe.

She took in several deep breaths, releasing them only after holding for a few seconds.

She debated whether or not she should go back in to the office to try and fix the situation, but decided against it as she still felt too raw to engage in a meaningful conversation with Sean.

"Fuck this. I'm going home."

She threw her car into reverse and when she looked to the rearview mirror to begin backing up from the parking spot, she jumped in her seat at the sight of a strange man dressed all in black standing across the street. She wanted to look away but couldn't.

Talia found herself frozen in fear. The man's presence and odd dress left an uneasy pit in her stomach. Despite not seeing his eyes, she could feel his gaze and it went right through her, down to her bones and her soul. It left her wanting to cry.

Out of nowhere, Talia had a sharp pain arise in her lower abdomen in the general location of where her uterus used to be, and she discovered she could move again by leaning forward in agony, wincing and pressing her hands to her belly.

Confused, she said, "What the," but stopped as the pain intensified. She threw her head back, grimacing. For the briefest of moments, she glanced back into the rearview mirror, despite her fear. The man had disappeared.

Suddenly, the pain had dissipated. A minute later, her thoughts went back to the stranger. She turned around in her seat and peered through the back window of the car and found no one on the street, not the man in black, not anyone.

"Am I seeing things now? And how the hell can I be having uterine pain? I had a hysterectomy years ago. I need to take an Ambien and go back to bed."

Like many of the people in Blackwood, sleepless nights had become par for the course. But she did sleep. They all slept. What they didn't do was rest, and that was much worse. Their nights were spent falling asleep and waking up in what seemed like an instant, or falling asleep and dreaming of all the horrors of *The Great Burn* and the regrets of their lives prior to it. Either way, the toll was the same.

Talia shifted back around and left the parking lot in a hurry. With the day going the way it had been, she wanted nothing more than to get home and take a nice, hot bath before anything else unusual happened.

Once home, she made herself a hot green tea, placing the mug next to the bottle of sleeping pills on the kitchen counter. She spotted a notepad and a pen nearby, and it was then the words started to form in her mind. She picked up the pen and started to write.

Once she got all her feelings down, she signed the letter and reread it three times before folding it into thirds.

Time, she thought. *The next few days are going to be hard and we all could use some time to reflect. I'm just going to force it with Sean.*

She put the letter in her purse, intending to go back to the office after hours that day to leave the letter on her desk for Sean.

For the time being, her attention shifted to her tea and the bubble bath awaiting her. She left the pills untouched.

7

Sean took up residence on the edge of town, so if he needed anything before heading home, he'd have to stop. Along his route down Cooley Street was the only grocery store in town, the Food Mart. He stopped there on most nights to pick up food or drink, but mostly for the conversation with the store's manager, Sharon Hood.

They had grown up on the same street in Blackwood so they knew each other well. Sharon was three years younger, however, so they had different groups of friends growing up. That did not stop Sharon from being a little smitten with Sean in their youth. His brown wavy hair, his torn jeans and red flannel shirt. The maturity of an older boy also appealed to her. And he could drive. *So cool,* she had thought, and without really trying to be, he just ... was.

When Sean went to California for college, she was just starting her sophomore year in high school. They didn't see one another the entire summer beforehand, and as it turned out, would not do so again until he returned home for the funeral of Dr. Mayweather.

Her eyes lit up at the sight of Sean in the parking lot of Meyer Funeral Home that mournful Tuesday afternoon. The entire town turned out to pay respects to their beloved hometown doctor, including many that had left Blackwood.

Sean hadn't changed much, still handsome and thin, just more mature in demeanor. When Sharon approached, Sean smiled and they exchanged a hug. When Sean introduced his wife, Vera and their son, Gabe, Sharon put on a charming smile, but on the inside was disheartened. Even after so many years apart, she held a sliver of hope that maybe his sudden return might be her one chance at pursuing him.

She had married, divorced, remarried, divorced again, and never had children. Ultimately, she landed back in Blackwood, and she was happier for it.

Her first marriage sent her to Dallas, Texas with Mark, a cowboy of a guy, a rancher, in fact. Good looks, gruff, blue jeans and boots and a well-worn brown cowboy hat passed down from his father. He wanted a big family capable of running the ranch, a house full of kids, and a wife that would be a caretaker of the home and the family. He was a respectful and decent man that treated her well. After just a year, however, Sharon realized she had no interest in the kind of life she would have with Mark. There was nothing wrong with the lifestyle he offered her, she acknowledged, but deep down, it just wasn't what she wanted for herself. She fell so hard, so fast for Mark's kindness, his good looks, and his fire in the bedroom, that she never really stopped to think about what her life would truly be like with him long term. She laid all the fault on herself, which made it that much harder to leave. He would never understand, but Sharon knew he'd be happier with someone else that was better suited to the big Texas, big family lifestyle.

Needing to get as far away from Texas as she could, Sharon took a job as an office manager with a food distribution company based in Las Vegas, Nevada. She moved there within two weeks of leaving Mark and found a busy and fast-paced way of life that allowed her to move on quickly from her short marriage.

Sharon soon fell victim to the rebound relationship. Jacob was younger by five years and the complete opposite of Mark. He worked in accounting for the same company she did and she described him as cute and sweet in a nerdy kind of way that reminded her more of Sean, yet lacking his natural charisma.

They dated for six months and when the lease on her apartment neared renewal, Jacob proposed the idea of her moving in with him, and playfully, threw out the notion of marriage.

She saw no reason to decline. Outside of work, they had become inseparable, spending most evenings and weekends together, even vacationing in Lake Tahoe and Denver. She did not feel head-over-heels in love with Jacob, not in that lustful, carnal way she once had with Mark, but she figured there were different kinds of love and relationships, each with their own set of rules and feelings. So, she moved in, they eloped a few months later in the presence of a few friends from work, and a year passed without issue. It was then the kernels of doubt crept into Sharon's head once again. She hoped time would help her to discover the full meaning of happiness and a deeper love for Jacob, yet the fire she expected would ignite with the passage of time never sparked.

She let another year pass of living with an air of reluctance and self-loathing hovering around until finally, her change in demeanor became so obvious that Jacob brought it up. She revealed her true feelings and to her surprise, Jacob wanted no part of a half-hearted relationship. The process took five days. They broke up, Jacob moved out, and once again, Sharon found herself wondering if she could or should ever really be with someone again.

At work, she endured the judgmental eyes and murmuring in the hallways. Clearly, everyone had taken Jacob's side in the breakup and divorce. Her thoughts turned to home, to Blackwood, a place she longed to escape from in her youth but could no longer steer away from as her Vegas life soiled. After a few phone calls, she had a job setup at the local grocery store as produce manager. A month later, she was home again. She steered clear of the men in town, instead choosing to focus solely on her career. It wasn't long before she took over as Store Manager.

Like most people in town, *The Great Burn* left her sort of floating through the days of her life, unsure what the future held, the only real thing being the nightmares and the trauma. Her subtle pursuit of Sean was the only positive emotion she felt on an average day.

The crisp white of the fluorescents at the less than cleverly named Food Mart bore down on Sean as he entered through the automatic door. The store was still and quiet save for the instrumental music playing overhead. There were only 13 aisles, not including the exterior walls that had the produce, deli, meat, and dairy sections. Small, but just right for Blackwood. Just past the four registers near the front of the store sat an elevated office area they called the bullpen. Generally, the manager on duty worked from there: overseeing the checkout, answering phones, making the schedule, among other things. The spot made it perfect for

Sean and Sharon to have daily conversations without seeking each other out.

Sean picked up a red shopping basket as he entered and meandered through the produce. After his dream about Gabriel and then his fight with Talia, he didn't have much of an appetite.

"What I really want is a stiff drink and a lobotomy," he quietly mouthed.

"Well, I think we can accommodate the drink, but I don't think you can get lobotomies anymore," Sharon said from behind Sean, startling him into spinning around.

His face turned red with embarrassment. He was sure no one heard him, but then again, he had no idea Sharon had snuck up behind him.

"Christ, you scared me."

"Sorry," Sharon said with a half-smile.

"And yes," Sean said, "they still do them, just not for my kind of problem."

"You doing all right? You look more ... haggard than normal."

"Oh, the usual. Insomnia. And when I do sleep, bad dreams. Ya know?"

She did. Most of the remaining residents of Blackwood knew it too. In the time since the flames tore their lives apart, each day seemed to pass with a stagnant indifference, in the ants marching kind of way. Each person dealt with their losses in often dramatically diverse ways, but the common thread amongst all the leftover people of Blackwood was the nightmares. Late at night, alone and at home in the dark, memories could do nothing but surface, ghosts could do nothing but haunt.

"Any thoughts about dinner?" Sharon inquired. "I've had a hankering for a frozen lasagna and I got a few bottles of wine.

Could be dinner for two?" Unconsciously, Sharon tossed her blonde bangs to the side and softly moistened her lips.

"Tempting, but I'm not hungry. I do appreciate the offer though. Maybe some other time."

"I will hold you to that eventually."

They smile at one another knowing they had done that same dance for months, always with the same result. The pain of losing Vera and Gabriel was still too close to his heart, though lately, most of his anxiety stemmed from the memories of his son.

"It is good to see you, Sharon, as always. I'm just gonna grab a few limes, some Canada Dry, and a bottle of gin, and maybe ... just maybe get some sleep tonight. I might pop into the diner tomorrow for lunch if you can join me."

"It's a date," Sharon blurted out. She covered her mouth in embarrassment.

"Well, it's a something." Sean spotted the citrus bins, pointed, and started walking that way.

"Bye, Sean," Sharon said, a little embarrassed.

8

Sean placed his grocery bag on the kitchen counter, removed everything, and lined up each item on the counter in the order he would assemble the drink. He sliced his lime and poured his gin and tonic, plopping three ice cubes in the glass at the end.

In the living room, Sean sat on the right side of the black leather sofa, as he always did, facing the massive picture window. He kept the beverage in his hand, sipping it while staring off into nothing. An hour had passed without him realizing it.

The sun had finally settled to the horizon, spraying cerise and maize across the town, and making the interior of the home dark. The long driveway and the country road were still visible through the large picture window but barely. At all times, day and night, even while away, Sean left the curtains drawn. He feared nothing after *The Great Burn* because he figured what's the worst thing that could happen. He didn't want to die, not exactly, but he felt a strong indifference. Besides, in a small town like Blackwood, nobody really locked their doors. Leaving a curtain open wasn't going to make much of a difference.

Sean stood from the couch, tired in his body, tired in his soul. As he turned to walk back to the kitchen for another drink, he caught sight of the five by seven picture frame on the entry table. He took the photo of Vera and Gabriel while they visited the Bronx Zoo a few weeks before he was notified of Dr. Mayweather's passing. Vera smiled wide, happiness beaming from her like rays of sunshine. It was the last time he remembered her being that happy.

Their time in Blackwood was disgruntled and generally miserable. Neither of them wanted to move away from New York, and the discussions before they did were never-ending, tense, and often induced tears in both of them. Ultimately, Sean convinced her to go, but it came with stipulations, the biggest being, if after four or five years they couldn't make it work, they would leave and come back to New York. They never got close to that timeframe. His wife and son were gone, but in a way he never could have predicted, not in a million guesses.

He walked over and picked up the photo, something he found in a plastic tote after their deaths. Vera's smile brought instant tears to his eyes. He longed to see her face again, joyful and full of hope, but unfortunately, the anger and bitterness of their last encounters is what lingered.

Sean slammed the frame face down onto the table and continued to the kitchen where he made another drink. Upon returning to the living room, he sat again, drink in hand, his lip quivering.

"I'm sorry, Vera. I'm sorry."

He gulped half his mixed drink.

"We never should have come back here." Sean closed his eyes, chugged the rest of his drink, and longed for a good night's sleep without the dreams. A sharp pain in his forehead suddenly surfaced. He rubbed the spot with this right hand. He assumed the alcohol was to blame.

Sean returned to the kitchen, placed his glass in the sink, found some aspirin, swallowed it dry, then decided it was time for a long, hot shower and some reading in bed.

Outside, near the end of the driveway and just out of the street, the stranger in black stood stoic, watching Sean from the shadows. He had plans for the doctor, but not that night. The time would come soon enough.

The interloper had already chosen his first target, a man who had lost more than anyone, a man who was more than ready to join his loved ones.

9

In the evening hours, Overton was mostly quiet and still for the residents. Though brightly lit at the nurse's stations and in the hallways, the rooms were dark. Some had the faint glow of a tv still on as the residents fell asleep. Some even had a radio playing softly.

Room 45 was no exception. Being as how the room was occupied by a comatose resident, the tv rarely played, the radio the same. From time to time, someone would sit and read to the man, or maybe sing, but it usually remained quiet and peaceful. The inner experience of the man in Room 45, however, was entirely different. His brain often fired on all cylinders just as if he were fully awake and conscious.

One of the main reasons the man had been kept alive was because of his high brain activity. He had been studied on numerous occasions, hooked up to odd looking helmets made of electrodes and white wiring, all to see how well his neurons were firing. It was determined early on that the man's mind was active and functioning, and from time to time, at very high levels, much like he was living a normal life. The problem, however, remained. Those functions did not pass from his mind to his body. During many days and nights, the man appeared to live a dynamic life, but it was only in his head.

That night was especially active. Lucid and aware, he walked down the street of a town that seemed familiar. The air was warm and dry. The street was mostly dark with a few house lights on and no traffic.

As he approached a house, he could feel another presence that stopped him in his tracks. There was no fear, just trepidation. He could feel the particles in the air stirring. He had no idea what to expect, only that he could feel he had stepped into a place perhaps he didn't belong.

He closed his eyes for a moment and when he opened them, he saw a flash of light and it was morning. After a moment of disorientation, the man looked around for clues to his location. It was the same street he had just been on, though a different day and time.

The air was smoky and thick. Fires raged all over the neighborhood. Many of the trees had blown down or had been broken in half, leaving smoldering branches scattered all over the yards and in the street. A hundred yards away, a charred and tilted fire hydrant spewed water into a nearby car whose windows had blown out.

The smell in the air hit the man in the way a long-lost memory does. He had been there before, many times, perhaps recently, perhaps a lifetime ago. The memory was suddenly not a pleasant one and it left him with a knot in his stomach.

A flash of light.

And the man was back on the street at night where he had originally appeared. A shadow in the form of man passed in front of him and headed toward the house to his right. Despite being startled, he managed not to jump back. The stranger did not acknowledge his presence. He followed the shadow with his eyes as it approached the sidewalk in front of the house.

After staying on that sidewalk for a few minutes without movement, a voice could be heard from inside the home. The words were indiscernible.

Another flash of light and the man was in a completely new location. He could tell he was on his back on the ground. It's daytime and the sky was hazy and smoky. A few seconds later, a burst of extreme heat enveloped his body and cut the breathable air. His skin bubbled from the heat as the pain crept into his nervous system. He screamed in agony. Then darkness.

10

Phil flopped down in his favorite recliner, the tan fabric mostly worn and tattered. The chair was a gift from Hanna on their fifth wedding anniversary. Since her death, Phil had spent as much time in that recliner as out of it, often passing out there after each night's drinking.

Worn out and dazed, Phil leaned forward and rubbed his eyes with both hands. He sighed heavy, unsure as to whether he needed a drink or needed a nap. One thing was certain - he was glad to be home.

The single-story craftsman style home sat narrow and deep on the lot. The offset front entrance led straight into the living room, with the dining area and kitchen behind that. The archway to the right of the dining room was the only access to the three small bedrooms and the one bathroom. A small winding staircase at the back of the kitchen lead upstairs to small bedroom suite in what used to be the attic space. It served as Phil and Hanna's master bedroom, although Phil had not used it since *The Great Burn*, instead choosing to use his mother-in-law Wilma's old bedroom.

Phil, Hanna, and their four children stayed in the house while caring for Hanna's mother during her final days, eventually taking ownership. They loved the house, though a little small for a growing family. Quaint, timeless, and in need of a little work, it was exactly what they would have bought had they ever chosen to.

Busy with life, the house remained mostly neglected during the family's time there. And, with no updates for about fifteen years before that, the house was in desperate need of a makeover. In Phil's current state, the house would likely never receive the care and attention it deserved.

"Is there anything I can get you before I head over to the shop?" Toby asked, but he already knew the first answer that would come.

"There's a bottle of whiskey in the cabinet next to the fridge. We can start with that."

Toby smirked. He rarely gave Phil any grief about the drinking, but considering they had just returned from the doctor's office, he decided it was an appropriate time to do so.

"You sure I can't just get you some coffee? Or maybe you should go lay down and rest."

Phil leaned back and kicked out his recliner with a loud clank. He shook his head vigorously at Toby's suggestions.

"Boss, we don't even know what's wrong with you yet. Best not aggravate that situation. Don't ya think?"

Phil leaned even further back and looked at the ceiling trying to find patterns in the popcorn texture. He failed to respond to Toby's concerns.

"Fine. Well, I'm not gonna help you do more damage to yourself. You can do that on your own." With his firm refusal to grab the booze, Toby turned to walk out and go to work. At the doorway, he turned back. "I'll be here tomorrow at the usual time to pick you up." Toby was fed up. When things got tough, he lost all sympathy for Phil's woes and it flooded his words. "Try not to kill yourself." He exited the house, slamming the door behind him."

Phil waved him off but instantly regretted leaving Toby in such a state. He thought about where he'd be without him. Probably dead. Definitely homeless and destitute.

"Damn it," Phil spoke softly.

He forced the lever down on his chair, gingerly rose, and made his way to the kitchen. From the cabinet he removed one of the seven brand new bottles of whiskey, twisted off the cap, and then tossed the cap across the room in the general vicinity of the trash can. There were six other caps strewn around the area and one empty bottle standing upright. The trashcan was empty.

He drank about twenty-five percent of the bottle just standing in the kitchen for five minutes. As he started to lose the feeling in his legs, he staggered back to his chair where he returned to his reclined position, bottle securely in his left hand, cradled between his thigh and the arm rest. In a haze of middling consciousness, four hours passed without any movement from Phil. No talking, no drinking.

His mind ran senseless through waves of horror, euphoria, and nothingness, drifting in and out of his memory. He lingered on the day of Hanna's car accident.

For the first time in two years, Phil and Hanna had arranged for an overnight babysitter for the kids. The years of taking care of Hanna's mother and the hectic day-to-day of raising four kids had left Phil and Hanna frazzled and disconnected. They were so excited for their little getaway; they could barely sleep the night before.

The drive from Blackwood was made considerably more attractive by the soft-top convertible Phil rented for the trip. They flew down the freeway like two teenagers running away from home, their cares and responsibilities left behind, only the moment they were living in on their minds.

"Grab that bag out of the glovebox, babe," Phil said, pointing.

"What is it?" Hanna asked as she reached forward to pull the lever. Inside, she spotted a plastic zip bag. She pulled it out and dangled it front of her face to get a better view of the contents. Six pre-rolled joints sat in the bottom of the bag.

"It's party time," Phil said in delight.

"I don't know," Hanna said, a bit reluctant about smoking pot on the road. She hadn't touched the stuff since before the kids were all born. "And where did you get this?"

"Some kid hanging out near the basketball courts at the high school."

"Never mind," Hanna put her hand up. "I don't want to know."

"Come on, babe, let's have some fun. We might not get another one of these rendezvous for a while. Go on, go on. Pull one out and spark it up."

Still hesitant, Hanna opened the bag and instantly pulled her head back at the wave of odor that blossomed into the car. She coughed a little. "God damn, Phil. This shit is strong."

"Oh yeah. Light one up and pass it over." Phil came prepared. He dug into his right front jeans pocket and pulled out a lighter, presenting it to Hanna.

She took it, removed one joint from the bag, sealed up the zipper, and placed it back in the glovebox.

With the lighter in her right hand and the joint in her left, Hanna flicked the wheel. The tiny flame was just enough fire to start the burn. She carefully passed the joint to Phil, who took it between his right index finger and thumb.

He took one short puff followed by a second longer one, letting it swirl inside before blowing it out. He gasped slightly afterwards but kept it together.

"Whoa! Fuckity fuck!" Phil yelled as he passed the joint back to Hanna. "These damn high school dealers got the good shit. Woo. When we were young, we'd be lucky to get ditch weed."

Based on Phil's reaction, Hanna hesitated to take a toke, but suddenly decided the stick up her ass had to go. She went for a tiny inhale at first and blew it out quickly, a test run of sorts. She felt a surge of energy, then the feeling her brain had detached itself from her head and started to float away before quickly reattaching itself. She took a second hit, a little longer than the previous time. With her eyes closed, she leaned back in the seat and let her head rest, taking in the air of the road as they traveled. For a brief moment, she questioned the potency of the weed. She'd never felt so high so fast. The thought passed as she fell deeper into the trip.

Meanwhile, Phil, also lost in an entirely separate world of psychedelic wonder, understood immediately they had gotten ahold of some rainbow weed. He remained fixed on the road ahead but his foot slowly pressed the gas pedal harder and harder until his speed became dangerous. To him, they were traveling in a tunnel of swiftly moving light. He also experienced the sensation that his head left his body, floating like a balloon just above his shoulders.

"Mind if I play some music, babe?" Phil asked as he turned on the radio and cranked the volume. Hanna did not answer.

His favorite classic rock station was playing Born to Be Wild by Steppenwolf.

Hanna put her hand out of the window and lost the joint. She saw her fingers like gelatinous masses, no longer able to grab hold of anything. She started to freak out. "My hands are Jell-o. Lime Jell-o. I wish they were strawberry. I'd eat those. I don't like lime. Phil." He didn't respond. "Phil! Did you hear me?"

He was no longer connected to the real world. The speedometer read ninety miles an hour and was climbing.

From their altered states, they could feel a sudden change in speed, their bodies jerking forward, then spinning and spinning and spinning. They lacked the awareness to understand what was happening. After a few seconds, dark.

Phil had little memory of the ambulance ride to Albuquerque. He remembered being on his back, brightly lit hallways, hearing hospital beeps, and the odor of ammonia. He could vaguely recall shouting out his wife's name. He remembered a doctor telling him his wife was gone, his own stoic reaction and looking down to find his hands shaking. From a few hours later, he remembered someone taking him down to the morgue in a wheelchair and seeing the lump of flesh and bones that used to be his wife under the crisp, white sheet, how cold her face was on his fingertips, and how utterly stupid he felt. Despite her body resting right before his eyes, the moment seemed unreal and confusing. His mind held no ability to process the truth of the situation. Only later on the phone with Toby did the reality hit him. After telling him what happened, he bawled uncontrollably for five minutes, finally hanging up the phone until he calmed down.

Most of the details of that day and the ones shortly thereafter were lost to Phil. The image of his wife on the slab is what stuck with him, burned into his head like the brand from a cattle rancher. He couldn't even recall the conversations he had with his children when he had to tell them what happened. It was just too difficult to go there. Drinking soon became the only way he could find to cope with his monumental loss and mistake.

Phil opened his eyes with his mind still on Hanna and her lifeless, mangled body. The whisky bottle was still firmly in his grasp. To further escape his past, he chugged another quarter of the bottle. His eyelids immediately started twitching back, his body grew numb again, this time deeper and faster. He teared up with his eyes already bloodshot. Nausea began to settle in. He took slow, deep breaths to keep it at bay. Two minutes later, he dropped the bottle at the side of his chair and passed out. Somehow, he avoided throwing up.

The day turned to night in the blink of a drunken eye. The clock on the wall showed 9:33, and with the house so quiet, the only sound was the ticking of that clock.

Unbeknownst to Phil, the stranger, whose presence earlier in the day coincided with his odd catatonic episode, stood on the sidewalk right outside his home, peering into the open front windows, waiting. A few seconds later, the man was no longer there. He didn't move, he was just ... gone.

Phil jerked in his chair, opening his eyes at a rustling in the bushes beneath the front windows. He didn't really know what he heard, only that he was reacting to a sound. Once his eyes adjusted to the darkness, he looked around the room but saw nothing out of the ordinary. Out of the corner is eye, a shadow shot past the windows, blending into the night. The fog of the booze had lifted somewhat, at least enough for Phil to know the difference between his imagination and the real world.

"Hey asshole! If you're gonna break in my house, at least wait and do it while I'm at work," Phil shouted.

He stayed quiet for a moment, looking and listening for movement. The bushes danced again, prompting Phil to rise and charge the front door. It had been a while since he felt actual fear, an emotion he understood to originate from having something to lose. With his wife and children dead, he deemed his own life forfeit. Nothing to lose, nothing to fear.

He turned the knob and threw it open in hopes of surprising the would-be intruder. "Boo!" Phil spat, then he waited. Suddenly, a gray and black ball of fur with glowing eyes scurried from the hedge line running straight away from the house, crossing the street and disappearing into the darkness. Phil's heart rate jumped a tad. "Stupid raccoons." He rolled his eyes and sighed, turned, walked back into the house, and slammed the door behind him.

He popped up the switch to his left, turning on the only living room light - a ceiling fan and three-light combo at the center of the room. The wicker inserts in the blades of the fan were discolored and tattered in many places. The illumination shone soft yellow, one of the bulbs flickering every five or six seconds. The near strobe effect gave Phil a headache.

As the details of the room became clear, he spotted the bottle he had dropped next to his chair, what was left of its contents now on the floor, the sight of which sparked his thirst.

"I need a fuckin' drink." Ready to begin a new bottle, he left the old one on the ground and headed for the kitchen.

Six steps from the kitchen entrance, Phil nearly jumped out of his skin when the front door flew open, rattling the house. The noise startled him but he wasn't scared. In that moment, something had settled deep inside of Phil. Without having the words for it, he understood the time had come for him to move on. There was no meaning in his continued existence, and the stranger in town might provide a means to an end.

Phil turned his body halfway around and used only his eyes to glance at the open door. He expected to see someone, but oddly enough, only the blackness of the night prevailed.

"You might as well come in. I'm gonna get a drink. You want one?" Phil tipped his head toward the kitchen to indicate where he was going. Before Phil could fully turn away, something emerged from the dark.

With the man in black's first step through the doorway, the living room lights flickered and a fierce wind blew through the room sending loose papers into the air. All the furniture rumbled in place. An empty booze bottle from weeks ago toppled from the coffee table, landing softly on the carpet.

Phil almost lost his balance but placing his hand on the wall helped him to avoid falling over.

The stranger took another quiet step in, this time causing the lights to max out their brightness before sparking and fading to nothing. The wind stopped at the same time. The man stood five feet past the threshold, and with a slight elevation of his hand, the front door slammed shut behind him.

Phil stepped backward to the kitchen. He hit the light switch up and down four times but got no results. He desperately wanted one last drink. *It never hurts to ask*, he thought.

"Hey buddy, how 'bout one last drink, for the road?"

The man did not speak but Phil's mind became filled with words and thoughts, inaudible answers to questions Phil had about the stranger and the past. Ideas about forgiveness and guilt and letting go of the pain swirled around. Then the visual memories took hold.

Sadness beset Phil. He rubbed the back of his right hand at the corner of each of his eyes as they teared up. He saw himself and his wife in the car on their way to Albuquerque for that weekend getaway.

Despite wearing a seatbelt, Hanna took the blunt of the impact. The entire right side of her body was crushed, her head hitting and shattered the side window. For his part, Phil suffered only minor whiplash and a few cuts and bruises.

His mind jumped again to his wife's body on the slab, then immediately to his children disintegrating to ash. He didn't witness the death of his children, and some part of him had always been grateful for that, but that didn't stop his mind from putting together a visual story that haunted him as much as an actual memory would have.

The odor of wood and flesh burning filled his nasal passages, gagging him and closing his throat. He peeled his eyes open to catch a glimpse of what the stranger was doing, but the man was no longer there.

A powerful noise, like the sound of a jet engine, erupted from the kitchen, sucking all of the air from the house.

Phil whipped around to find the stranger right behind him, his long, black duster pulled open, the inside resembling the entrance to a bottomless cavern. From that blackness emerged a fire the size of a match head and growing, and he was instantly taken back in time to *The Great Burn*. Because he often suffered from drunken hallucinations, Phil wasn't sure if what he was seeing was real or a terrifying waking dream. Sean's words about having a seizure came to mind, so Phil wondered if perhaps that was what he was experiencing. Regardless, he had no fight left in him, no will to live, the memories of everything he had lost finally taking the last shred of his soul.

As the fire grew, Phil chose not to resist the heat. He tipped his head back, closed his eyes, and allowed the wall of flame to take him. In an instant, Phil was gone.

The stranger then disappeared much like he had arrived. The only evidence of his presence was a small circle of black tar and soot where Phil once stood in the kitchen. That and the smell of an old campfire that had been left burning through the night.

11

Friday morning came like almost every weekday since they met. Toby arrived at Phil's house to pick him up for work, and maybe they'd have breakfast at The Empty Diner. The later was usually dependent on the amount of drink Phil consumed the night before. If it were a particularly rough evening, Toby would have to spend two hours just trying to get coffee down his bosses' throat, and that only after a thirty to forty-five-minute struggle with getting Phil showered and dressed.

If the demons took a break the night before and he could find a few hours of sleep with less drinking, Phil would wake up starving and ready for his crispy but not burnt bacon, two scrambled eggs, and white toast with extra butter. Those mornings had become rare, much to Toby's dismay.

After Thursday's odd events, Toby fully expected it to be a coffee and shower kind of morning, but he really wasn't in the mood for either. He left Phil's house the day before feeling quite pissed off at the man's lack of self-awareness.

Toby left his truck and walked the path to Phil's front door, his steps full of reluctance. He always felt guilty when he snapped at Phil. After everything his boss had gone through, surely, he was allowed some erratic behavior to mask his grieving, Toby often thought, but where does the line get drawn and how much time has to pass before life must continue with some semblance of normality? Toby didn't know the answer. He was certain no one in Blackwood did either.

Phil never locked his front door, so Toby did his usual double knock before walking right in. He was pleasantly surprised to not find Phil in the recliner, which could mean he was already awake or actually in bed.

There was just enough daylight in the house to see but not enough for Toby's liking. Toby hit the wall switch but nothing happened.

"Why should I expect him to have changed a light bulb?" Toby shook his head as he looked around.

The usual empty bottles littered the floor and there were newspaper pages and plastic grocery bags scattered all over the room. An odd combination of odors filled the air: whiskey and campfire. Toby spotted the knocked over bottle by the recliner that helped explain one smell. The other one and the garbage remained a mystery.

"Jesus, Phil. Did you leave the front door open last night?"

He stepped through the living room and into the kitchen. He stopped just short of the threshold when he spotted an ashy black circle on the floor. He tried the kitchen light and that failed too. The first thought that came to mind is that a circuit blew or the power was completely out.

Toby crouched down to get a closer look. The ash formed a perfectly circular pattern with an outward burst. He couldn't think of anything that might cause that pattern if it were dropped or left on the floor. It was too perfect. He stood up and went to the bedroom.

After a fruitless search, Toby went to the bathroom, and finally the other bedrooms. Phil was not in the house. Phil never left the house before Toby came by. Never.

Considering the medical issue Phil had experienced the day before, Toby wondered if something went wrong and if he had to return to the doctor.

"Someone would have called me, right? If Phil went to the hospital? I should probably just call Sean to make sure."

Toby left the house and made a quick sweep of the back and front yards before heading back to his car. Phil was nowhere to be found. Toby arrived at the driver side door in a mild state of panic. All he could think about was an image of Phil lying dead in a ditch somewhere.

As he pulled his keys from his pocket, a newer black sedan pulled up and parked on the opposite side of the street. Toby pretty well knew every person and every car in town, and this car was not from Blackwood. A man of Mexican descent emerged, average in height and weight, with perfect black hair, no facial hair, and a wrinkle free black suit, black tie, and white dress shirt. He was totally unknown to Toby. In that particular moment, the stranger's presence was odd, so Toby stood facing him.

The stranger left his vehicle and approached.

"Hey there. Everything okay? You seem a little ... sorted."

"You always just pull up and ask random people if they need help?"

"Well, yeah, most of the time."

Toby smirked at the idea.

"Sorry," the man said as he pulled identification from the inside pocket of his suit jacket. "Special Agent Angel Learza." He returned the ID to its place nearly as fast he brought it out.

"Special Agent, huh? I'm local mechanic Toby McNamee," he said with a bit of sarcasm as he tried to match the official sounding nature of Agent Learza's title. "What are you doing in Blackwood?"

"I'm tracking a case across state lines. Something led me here. I saw you as I came down the road and you looked a little distressed, so I stopped. Are you?"

"What?"

"Distressed? Is there anything I can help with?"

Toby thought about it for a moment. *Phil is missing. This guy is clearly some sort of law enforcement. The timing of his arrival is a little weird, but hey, fuck it. Maybe he could help.*

"My boss is missing."

"Oh? When's the last time you saw him?"

"Yesterday, mid-morning. He wasn't feeling well. He saw our local doctor, then I brought him home. Came to pick him up for work this morning," Toby pointed toward the house, "and he's nowhere to be found."

"Couldn't he have just gone somewhere?" Agent Learza shrugged his shoulders. "Gas station? Breakfast? Lots of reasons someone wouldn't be home."

"No. Not Phil. To be frank, he's a blackout drunk. I pick him up for work every day. It's been years since I didn't. In the last year, I don't think Phil has been anywhere except work, home, the diner, the gas station, and the grocery store."

"I see. I take it that's his house?"

"Yep. I was just about to head over to the local diner and see if anyone had seen or heard from him."

"That's a great idea. I tell you what," Agent Learza said as he pulled a business card from his left pants pocket, handing it to Toby, "give me a call if no one else has seen him or if you don't find him. I can check out the house, just to be certain. If that's okay with you?"

"Knock yourself out. The door is never locked, so you can go right in. Forgive the mess."

Agent Learza nodded.

Toby suddenly remembered everyone talking about a stranger in black standing across the street from The Empty Diner. He looked over the agent again, and though he was dressed mostly in black, he didn't fit the description at all. *So, what brought him to Blackwood?* Toby looked at the card. It had only two things on it, centered: *Learza*, and beneath that: *444-321-0001*.

"Just out of curiosity, what's this case that brought you to town? We don't get a lot law enforcement around here, but the reason I'm really asking is because there was some weirdo in town yesterday right before Phil got sick, and he was kind of freakin' everybody out."

"Hmmm. That's interesting. Active investigation though, so I can't really say more than that. Can you describe this person?"

"I didn't actually see him, but the others said he was tall, dressed all in black, had on a long black duster and a wide-brimmed hat. Pretty stupid for a hot day in August. Like I said, I was in the bathroom and didn't see the guy."

Agent Learza rubbed his chin and nodded lightly. "Okay, well, you have my card, so just give me call, even if you find your friend. That way I'll know whether we need to make something of this. I'll let you outta here then."

"Great. Thank you."

"Good to meet ya, Toby." Agent Learza put out a hand.

Toby shook it. "Same to you. I'll be in touch."

Toby hopped in his truck and drove away.

Agent Learza watched Toby drive away, then turned to face the house. Based on everything Toby had mentioned, he knew he was in the right place.

He entered the property with cautious steps. Just like Toby had, he found the lights not working and no sign of Phil anywhere. He made a mental note of the empty booze bottles, the debris, the general lack of cleanliness, and the family photos showing Phil, his wife, and their four kids. It was obvious Phil lived in the house alone, which helped to explain the alcoholism and state of the house. Clearly, Phil had lost control of his life and was spiraling to nowhere.

When he reached the kitchen, Agent Learza used a small flashlight pulled from his pocket to get a good look at the ash mark on the floor. Rather than having the sense of confusion held by Toby when he saw it, Agent Learza studied it for just a moment, then nodded like he had just confirmed a previous thought.

Agent Learza had been sent to put a case to rest, and with everything he had seen and heard so far, his confidence swelled. He left the area as mysteriously as he had arrived.

12

Sean awoke unsure how much he had actually slept. On most days, he couldn't recall being awake all night, but he was always left with the distinct impression he hadn't slept. Most insomniacs experience a kind of waking sleep where they aren't asleep but aren't awake either – a conscious coma, Sean often called to it.

He slogged to the bathroom for his morning routine which included standing in a hot shower for fifteen minutes to wake up his muscles and clear out his sinuses. He decided to leave his beard and mustache scruff with his mind already on the weekend.

Looking in the mirror, Sean said, "This is the beginning of the end for you, Sean. When you stop caring about your appearance, you'll stop caring about everything. Next thing, you'll be eating french fries at every meal."

He turned his head left and right, looking at the light facial hair growth. The last time he wore a beard and mustache was in medical school but this didn't remind him of that. There were tiny specks of gray in the color now. Distinguished, he thought, but lazy. He combed his hair to its usual laid-back look, got dressed in blue slacks, a white buttoned-down, long-sleeved shirt, and a tri-colored blue tie that matched his pants. His shoes were a somewhat pointy brown dress shoe from Cole Haan that Vera had bought him two birthdays ago. He left the bathroom having doubts about the facial hair but let it go as he stepped to the kitchen.

Anticipating a less than ideal weekend of not eating enough and drinking too much to dull the pain of his memories, Sean decided to start his Friday morning off with a smoothie. Only problem might be in a lack of ingredients.

He opened the fridge and spotted a yogurt container. He grabbed it, pulled off the lid, and took a sniff. "Still good," he said. From the crisper drawer, he found small green baskets of blueberries, strawberries, and raspberries. Upon inspection, he tossed out the mushy and moldy strawberries and decided the others were still good enough to eat.

He gathered his blender and all the ingredients on the counter. He stood there just looking at them. Smoothies always reminded him of Vera. She made them nearly every morning before they left the house to work or to run. Sean was never much of a breakfast kind of person but she insisted on how important it was to start the day with something healthy.

Sean closed his eyes and the memory of the incident that would lead them from New York to Blackwood came to mind. It was painful to think about it. Vera and Gabe were gone, and he blamed himself because had they never moved to Blackwood, they would still be alive. He hated himself for that. On most days, he wished he had perished with them.

Sean often thought about the chain of events that brought him back to his hometown of Blackwood. The guilt ground his mind to pulp nearly every day since *The Great Burn*, survivor's guilt and all that, but even more so because of the initial resistance his wife communicated over the idea of moving from Manhattan. She had spent her entire life in the trenches of New York City. They had met, fallen in love, gotten married, and started raising their son Gabriel there.

Upper Manhattan, New York – a few years ago

Sean entered the kitchen, his steps slow and unsteady, looking down at this cellphone, confounded and speechless. He stopped just inside the threshold. The last person in the world he could have imagined getting a phone call from was Janice Mayweather, let alone anyone from Blackwood. He had all but lost himself in the New York life he had built. He hadn't even thought about his hometown in months.

His wife Vera turned from stirring the boiling pasta she was preparing for dinner and sifted through a drawer on the island in search of the corkscrew. She hadn't noticed Sean enter the room, his footsteps so soft, his voice ... missing. When she looked up to grab the wine bottle in front of her, the guise on her husband's face made her stop moving except to place the corkscrew down on the counter.

"Sean? What's the matter? You're stark white."

Sean continued to stare at his phone but said nothing.

"Sean, honey. You're scaring me. What's wrong?"

He didn't immediately answer.

"Sean!"

Out of his trance, Sean finally looked up. "I ... um," he sputtered, his brow strained with deep thoughts.

Vera whipped around the island and met Sean face to face. "Sean, has something happened? What is it?" She cradled his right elbow and guided him gently to the dining room table and into the end chair. She looked him in his eyes. "Take a deep breath. Do it."

He looked right back into her eyes and followed orders.

"Take another one. Nice and slow, then let it out."

He did as he was instructed.

As calmly as she could, she said, "Now, tell me what the hell is going on or I'm going to start to freak out. I've had half a bottle of wine already while cooking dinner, so please talk to me." She pulled out a chair and sat down, grabbing his free hand in a kind embrace.

"Harold Mayweather passed away," Sean said emotionless, still in shock.

Vera knew the name but it took her a second to rattle out her full knowledge of him. She ran her free hand through her hair and gripped Sean's hand tighter. "Oh, babe. I'm so sorry."

Sean shook his head and placed his phone face down on the table. He craned his neck back and stared at the ceiling and let out a sigh. Dr. Harold Mayweather had been his mentor, a father-figure, and a great friend. Sean pulled his head back down and looked to his wife, his eyes cavernous, his mind scrambling around a million thoughts.

"I know how much he meant to you. What happened? He had to be pretty old, right?"

"Yeah, I think he was in his mid-eighties, maybe. Can't remember anymore. It's been too long. Wow." Sean took in a long, hard breath and sighed again on the exhale. "He uh, died in his sleep. They think heart attack. Won't know for sure until the autopsy comes back."

Vera moved to a position behind Sean and rubbed his shoulders for a few minutes. She kissed his head and went back to the stove to finish their dinner. After turning off the stove burner and removing the cork from the bottle, she poured Sean a full glass of wine, walked over to him, and put it in his right hand.

"Drink." She returned to the pot of pasta to drain the water.

He wasn't sure he wanted to be numb. He hadn't even fully processed the news. Sean looked to his wife with doubt in his eyes.

"Drink it, Sean. You can sort out your feelings later." She knew him well enough to know what he was thinking in that moment. "Right now, you need to relax. Drink it all."

Sean took a sip, letting it settle on his tongue before swallowing. The taste was pleasant, fruity and balanced, a little dry. He took another drink, bigger this time, then one more to finish off the glass. He rose from his seat, walked over to the island, grabbed the wine from the counter, and attempted to finish it off straight from the bottle but fell about a glass short.

He could feel his mind drift, his eyes weighing down. Sean was only a casual drinker, so the wine made quick work. He raised a hand to his cheek, then to his forehead. His skin had turned a bit red and was hot to the touch. He lost all thought of Dr. Mayweather, his attention turning to their son.

"Where's Gabe?" Sean asked.

As she finished prepping the meal, Vera said, "Katy's on her way here. Remember? Gabe and Brodie had a play date." She looked to Sean and caught him swaying where he stood. "You need to sit down before you fall down."

Vera came around the island and walked Sean back to a chair at the table. The doorbell rang. "Sit tight. We're going to eat as soon as Gabe gets settled."

Vera left the room. Five minutes later, she and Gabe returned to the kitchen. Vera went to the counter, grabbed the food, and brought it to the table, placing the bowls in the center.

Gabe, with his short, brown curly hair and endless curiosity and observation skills, went to his father's side and instantly questioned his condition.

"Daddy? Why is your face so red?"

"Gabe, go wash your hands," Vera commanded. "It's time for dinner."

Gabe looked to his mother then immediately back to his father.

"Now, Gabe," Vera commanded in a much deeper and serious tone.

He obeyed, shuffling down the hall to the bathroom.

When the boy returned, he joined his parents at the table for dinner. Gabe and Vera spoke about his day at school and his time spent with his friend Brodie.

Sean said nothing, picking lightly at the food on his plate, never really taking a full bite. His mind had returned to Dr. Mayweather and his hometown of Blackwood as he sat at the table.

An hour later while soaking in a bath, he tipped his head back and shed a long continuous stream of tears just from the corners of his eyes, a soft whimper the only sound he could muster from quivering lips.

A few hours later after bathing his son and reading a story to him before bed, Sean called it night but tossed and turned for hours, finally falling asleep at 3 a.m.

A morning run in Manhattan had become a part of his daily routine. Sean couldn't even remember the last time he missed a day. That morning, however, was different. His feet were heavy, his steps clunky, but only in the beginning. As he went on, his flow eased and the weight shifted to his shoulders.

Faster and faster he ran, like someone or something was chasing him and he needed to get as far away from it as humanly possible. He had no ill will in regards to his past life in Blackwood. Growing up there was a mostly positive experience and he loved the town and the people, but his spirit had longed for something bigger and more impactful. Once he left, he believed he was gone for good.

His mother had died from breast cancer when he was eight years old and he was raised by his father, who never remarried. When Sean went to college, his father moved to Florida, later passing away from a massive heart attack when Sean was in his first year of medical school.

For the first time since he left, Sean had a reason to return to Blackwood. Paying his respects to Dr. Mayweather felt like the right thing to do. Oddly enough, everything in his mind, body, and spirit made him want to run away. It didn't make much sense, but nonetheless, there was a desperation in the way he ran that morning.

Two blocks away from returning to home, Sean stopped running and began his walking cooldown. The sidewalks and streets were busy with the typical traffic and bustling of the morning. Near a bus stop bench, a homeless man sat on the curb facing the street. He held a sign over his head and was shifting it slowly from left to right, attempting to draw the attention of the people driving by. Sean had a five-dollar bill in his sweatpants pocket, so he pulled it out assuming the man's sign was some message asking for food or money.

Sean stepped to just behind the man. "Here you go buddy."

The man did not turn around. "I don't need that, Doc."

Sean withdrew the money, a furrowed brow displaying his confusion. "Do I know you?"

The man turned the sign around so Sean could read it, but he stayed facing the street. The sign read: The End is Nigh.

Sean chuckled a little. "Not very original there, bud."

"But true ... at least for you."

Tired of the game, Sean reached over the man's shoulder and dropped the five bucks in his lap. As he pulled his arm back, the homeless man dropped the sign and grabbed Sean's arm at the wrist, turned to face him, and pulled him close.

Sean saw his eyes were deformed and it became obvious the man was blind.

"Don't go back there, doc!" The homeless man shouted through a mouth half-full of rotten teeth. "Death waits there. The end is nigh."

"Let go of my arm," Sean said in defiance, easily twisting his way free of the man's grasp. Sean walked briskly toward home. About twenty steps away, he glanced back and found the man had disappeared from the curb.

Sean shook his head and kept walking. "Like I don't have enough shit to worry about right now. Jesus."

A few days after getting the visitation and funeral details from Janice Mayweather, Dr. Mayweather's widow, Sean booked the travel for his visit to Blackwood. Vera decided she wanted to come along and bring Gabe. She relished the opportunity to see the place Sean had grown up. All she knew of him was the New York, big city doctor version. She almost couldn't wrap her head around the idea that he came from a small southwestern rural town. She always knew about his upbringing, of course, but she had never thought much of it until the moment they were planning the trip.

While they sat at Sean's office computer booking the airline tickets, Vera asked, "So, how many people actually live in Blackwood?"

"Ummm ... I'm not exactly sure. I don't think it was more than a thousand or two when I was there. I have no idea if it's grown or not."

"Wow. There's probably more people living on this block."

"There might be damn near as many living in this building."

He thought about where they might stay while in town. An internet search revealed a Comfort Inn and a Holiday Inn Express just off the freeway but they would be twenty miles away. There appeared to be no choice. Blackwood had no hotel, no shitty roadside motel, not even a bed and breakfast.

"Babe, just so you know, the uhhh, accommodations are going to be a little ... low class compared to what we're used to. It's really too far to drive in and out of town from Albuquerque. The closest hotel is twenty miles away, and it's the kind with no room service and powdered eggs for breakfast, and most likely, the coffee is going to be somewhere between piss and hotdog water."

"Hey, I think I can handle a few days away from New York."

"We live in Manhattan. That's a bit different than just saying New York."

"I wasn't born with a silver spoon up my ass," Vera said, growing a little agitated by Sean's implications.

"Well, you have one firmly planted there now," Sean joked.

Vera playfully slapped the back of Sean's head. "You dick. When's the last time you went into a mom-and-pop diner and got a normal cup of coffee instead of an expresso? Hypocrite."

"I was joking, Jesus."

"You're mean. And I'll be fine," Vera looked down at the computer screen, "at the Holiday Inn. If the coffee sucks, we'll just go to Starbucks every morning."

He decided not to tell her the truth about that idea. In her world, there was a Starbucks on every corner. Near Blackwood, there wasn't one within a hundred miles. The idea did get him thinking about the things he missed about his hometown, the diner being one of them. He hoped it was still open.

As a teen, he spent his fair share of time hanging out there after football games, drinking sodas and sharing huge plates of fries or nachos with his friends. It brought a smile to his face.

In those days, The Empty Diner was owned and operated by a local husband and wife, Javier and Rose Vargas, who retired and sold the business while Sean was in medical school. They were extra tolerant of the teens when they hung out, often employing many of them part-time to help with dishes and cleaning the bathrooms. The best food they served was a cheesy omelet topped with salsa for breakfast and Taco Tuesdays where they offered a special day of authentic Mexican meals from recipes their grandmothers taught them. That was always their busiest day of the week.

Sean only hoped the restaurant held the same spirit and character it held in his younger days, and that Vera would discover this for herself, despite expecting to only be in town for a few days.

13

The pain in his lower abdomen had become unbearable. His mind screamed in agony for the aching to end, but no one could hear him. The comatose man lived all his experiences, his thoughts, his joy and sadness, and every ounce of fear and pain in the darkness of his mind. All he could focus on was wanting it to end.

He suddenly appeared in an unfamiliar doctor's office, witnessing a medical procedure being done on a woman. Based on what he could see, the man understood instantly he was witnessing a fetal extraction.

As fast as he had arrived, he was transported away to a new place where the same woman sat on the edge of a bed, sobbing with both her hands overlapping on her lower abdomen.

In the blink of an eye, the comatose man disappeared and reemerged in another doctor's office. The same woman, although a little older, stood behind a desk with a letter in her hand, deep in thought, concern in her eyes.

The man then felt a presence just behind him, one the woman noticed. She locked eyes in his direction but she was no longer concerned. Acceptance was the only word the comatose man could use to describe her eyes and body language in that moment.

The world grew dark once again, the pain in his abdomen gone. He pondered what his recent out of body experiences meant and why he was having them. They were unlike anything he had gone through before and he felt there might be a purpose behind them. Before long, he once again lost all sense of space and time.

14

Talia arrived at the office a full hour before she was scheduled to come in, parking behind the building so anyone who happened to drive by would not know she was present. She had no intentions of working that day. Her only purpose in showing up was to leave the note she had written for Sean.

Upon entering the building, she left the lights off and went straight to her desk. She removed the note from her purse and just stood there facing the entrance of the office. She had no doubts about leaving the letter, but she wondered what the future might hold for her personal and professional relationship with Sean.

She had been bitter for a short time after their fight but that subsided rather quickly and turned to despair. She never needed to be reminded of her past decisions, least of all from Sean. She lived with the pain of her betrayal to her husband Jorge every day, and with his death in *The Great Burn*, it had only become amplified. She could never see his face again, never kiss him again, and never get a chance to tell him the truth and hope they could work through the deception. That knowledge ate away at her like a festering and bubbling pool of acid.

Talia closed her eyes, took in a deep breath, and when she opened them, a figure stood in the lobby a few feet from the entrance. Despite the darkness of the room, she knew it was the stranger. She wanted to speak but found herself unable to. She held the letter in her right hand, elevated slightly above the keyboard on her desk.

A single tear fell from the corner of her left eye but she wasn't scared. A deep sense of relief washed over her body as the man in black slowly opened his long overcoat. Even from across the room, Talia could feel the heat emanating from the stranger. She closed her eyes again and soon vanished. The letter that she once held in her hand fell to the desk below like she had placed it there herself.

15

The streets of downtown Blackwood were quiet when Sean pulled up to The Empty Diner. The only other vehicle in the lot was Toby's truck. The day had started like every day in Blackwood. It was sunny. It was hot. It was desolate.

Good, Sean thought after seeing Toby's vehicle. *I can take a quick look at Phil.*

Upon entering the restaurant, Sean stopped for a moment to look around for Phil. There were three people present. Ted and Raelle stood behind the counter, both right in front of Toby who was seated there. They were deep in a discussion. Phil was not in sight.

Sean walked right up to the counter. "Phil in the bathroom?"

Toby turned to face Sean. "You got good timing. Actually, he's missing. We were just discussing where the hell he could be. You examined him yesterday. Could something ... medical have happened?"

"Whoa whoa whoa," Sean said, holding up his hand. "What do you mean missing?"

"Missing," Toby said. "Like, can't find him. I went to pick him up this morning for work and he was nowhere to be found."

"Jesus, he may have been having seizures. Did you check his house and property?"

"Of course. I go there every day to pick him up, and to be blunt, clean him up, if necessary. He was nowhere to be found."

"Is it possible he left and went somewhere? If he wandered off and had an episode, he could be lying in a ditch somewhere or collapsed on the street."

"I figured something like that was possible but I doubt he would have left the house," Toby said. "Once he starts drinking, that's all she wrote. He wouldn't have gone anywhere until I arrive in the morning. He can't drive. I take him everywhere."

"Okay then," Sean relented.

"Can I get you a coffee?" Raelle asked of Sean.

Sean nodded. "Thank you."

"Tell him about the agent," Ted chimes in.

"Yeah, here's the kicker. I come out of Phil's house and a black sedan pulls up. A guy in a black suit pops out and comes up and asks me if everything is okay. Real government spook type."

Raelle placed a coffee mug in front of Sean and poured.

Sean took a seat and emptied a single half and half into the coffee, stirring before taking a sip. Memories of all the great Manhattan coffee houses flooded his head. The word *average* came to mind, as it usually did when he had coffee outside of the home, but he never once said anything to Ted or Raelle. From his experiences, most diner coffee suffered from poor roasting, terrible bean to water ratios, and a lack of body and character. Then again, for a buck-fifty, he didn't expect any better.

"F.B.I. or something?" Sean asked.

"I guess. Special Agent. Whatever that means."

"He show you identification?"

"Yeah, but I didn't really pay much attention. Looked real. I was a little distracted dealing with the fact that Phil was MIA."

"Fair enough. So, what'd he say? Why was he there?" Sean took a few more sips of his coffee.

"Said he was investigating a case, couldn't give me any deets. I told him about Phil and the man in black from the street. He didn't say much. Gave me his card. Said to call him if we can't find Phil."

"So, let's just think logically about all this." Sean said. "Where did we last see Phil?"

"When I took him home after he saw you yesterday. That was the last time I saw Phil," Toby said. "Could he be passed out somewhere in town? I suppose so. I guess we could canvas the neighborhood."

"And then there's the matter of the stranger." Raelle said. "I honestly think that what happened to Phil ... what happened to all of us that saw him, was caused by that stranger." She received looks of incredulity from Ted and Sean. She waved them off. "You don't think I know how it sounds?" She finally decided to be honest. "But one second this guy shows up, the weather gets all disturbed, and then next thing you know, Ted's gotta bloody nose," she looked to Ted and pointed, "don't think I didn't notice." She continued, "I'm bent over and can't breathe, and Phil barfs up his breakfast and almost can't walk."

"Look," Sean said, "I don't know anything about a stranger but there has to be a more reasonable explanation for what happened. There's a million reasons why all of you could have been afflicted at the same time with similar symptoms."

"Name one," Ted said.

"Food poisoning," Sean rebutted.

"Oh, fuck you doc! You say I'm poisoning people now."

"No, Ted," Sean said.

"Calm down, Ted, Jesus," Raelle said, putting her hand on Ted's forearm. "No one is saying you're trying to kill us. Even the best food prep occasionally results in foodborne illness."

"Right," Sean agreed. "But I didn't mean from here necessarily. All I'm saying is that there must be some sort of more reasonable explanation for your ills that doesn't involve the supernatural."

"You weren't there, Sean," Raelle said. "I do tend to agree with you, but I felt something."

"Like a pain?" Sean asked.

"No, no. More like an energy. And not a good one."

Sean had no idea how to respond any further without belittling Raelle. He couldn't deny their experience. Clearly, something odd happened to them, but Sean could not make the leap she was attempting to.

"Should we call the sheriff?" Toby asked.

Ted started back toward the kitchen, speaking as he walked. "They won't do anything until someone's been missing for twenty-four hours. Waste of time at this point."

"He's right," Sean said. "I like Toby's idea of canvasing the neighborhood and any other locations he might normally go."

"And how do we go about doing that?" Toby asked.

"Considering he was likely drunk, we should start with the area and streets around Phil's house and spread out from there, kind of in an ever-expanding circle. Other than here, home, and work, does he go anywhere else?"

"Frank's gas station and sometimes the grocery store." Toby said. "That's about it."

Sean looked to his watch. It was 8:25. "Shit I gotta go. Office is open in five minutes." He grabbed his cup and downed the last of the coffee from it. "Raelle, can I get half a dozen of your cheese danishes and two large coffees to-go, please?"

"You bet." She turned around and began putting his order together.

"Here's my suggestion. Toby, if you want to check out Phil's local spots, go around and do so, otherwise, there isn't much the authorities or us are going to be able to do until tomorrow. I don't know what your workload looks like these days but if he hasn't turned up by this time tomorrow, I say we all get together and do a canvas.

"Nothing critical at the shop right now. If I need to close the shop tomorrow, it won't be a problem."

"Perfect."

Raelle poured two cups of coffee, placing the lids securely on them. She set the box of danishes and the two coffees in a dual carrier on the counter in front of Sean.

"How much?"

"On the house. Let's just hope Phil turns up so we can put this mess behind us."

Sean thought to argue but decided instead to just accept the gift and nod in appreciation.

Toby stood up and walked out with Sean.

At the head of their vehicles, Sean said, "Yeah, so just text me tomorrow if Phil is still missing, or at any time if you happen to find him."

"Alright doc. Talk to you then."

They waved to each other, got in their vehicles, and drove away.

On the short drive to his office, Sean thought about how he'd handle his apology to Talia for his asshole behavior the day before. He hoped the coffee and pastries would help. Until their argument the day before, he couldn't remember having a single heated exchange with her. She had been with him since the beginning of his days as Dr. Mayweather's replacement, and he knew that without her, he'd be lost. The idea crossed his mind of paying for her to take a vacation to some place where the sand came with ocean breezes and exotic cocktails instead of the dust in Blackwood that always came with painful memories and cheap beer.

I'll just have to see how it goes, he thought. *Maybe she won't even be that mad. Maybe.*

16

Sean arrived at the office at 8:35. Juggling his bag, the coffees, and the pastries, he attempted to open the front door only to find it locked. Talia almost always arrived at fifteen after eight to get the office open, which included unlocking the door, turning on the lights and the tv, and booting up the computer systems.

With the disappearance of Phil, the presence of a stranger in black, and the sudden arrival of an F.B.I. agent, Sean's mind went immediately to the possibility that something bad may have happened to Talia. He didn't want to jump to conclusions, however, as she may have just forgotten to unlock the door.

He peered through the darkened glass but couldn't really see any lights on or any movement.

"Okay. Calm down, Sean. There is a reasonable explanation for this." He took a deep breath. "These people got me thinking crazy."

Sean carefully placed the box on the sidewalk, then found his keys and unlocked the door. After picking up box, he turned around and used his butt to push the door open. The darkness of the room made it clear that no one was there.

He walked around to Talia's desk and put the coffee and pastries near the computer's keyboard. Even in the barely lit office, Sean noticed the yellow, folded piece of legal paper sitting on the keyboard with his name written on it in black sharpie marker.

Sean pulled out Talia's desk chair and placed his bag in the seat. He hesitated for a moment to pick up the note, a bit worried he might find a business-level Dear John letter. The rational side of him finally overcame his fear.

Dear Dr. Atwater,

"Shit. Here we go."

On most days, I can see in your eyes the pain you can't seem to shake, and you're right, I often suffer the same kind of feelings about my loss. Somehow, we both need to find a way to move on from the past. I'm not suggesting we forget because I know we never will, but I am saying we need to be able to function better. Every day here in Blackwood has started to feel exactly the same: a long trudge through muddy waters with no view in sight where it will end. If you ask me, that sounds a lot like a hell on Earth.

I've come to accept the past, as difficult as it's been, and you need to do the same or you may be destined to never really live again.

I would suggest closing the office for today and giving yourself some time to reflect.

Talia

"God damn it." Sean sighed. He grabbed his bag from the chair and tossed it onto the floor nearby before flopping into the chair. His guilt once again overwhelmed him, like it did nearly every day. He thought about her words, and how right she was that so many people had not seemed to find a way to move on, and how each day had become a broken record playing the same bar of the same song. He wondered if his missteps with Talia were just the thing needed to push the needle.

Sitting alone in the dark of his medical office, he felt alone and it only served to remind him of what he had lost in *The Great Burn*. In his dreams, he often heard the voice of his son, Gabe, but never Vera's. For that, he called her cellphone, the one he kept in his nightstand just to listen to her outgoing message. He used the office phone sitting on Talia's desk to dial the number and put the receiver to his head, his eyes already tearing up, his lips quivering.

"You've reached Vera's phone message, so that means I'm either busy or don't want to talk to you. Leave a message if you want."

In the background, the voice of a child could be heard using indiscernible words and then giggling.

Abruptly, the message cut off with the sound of loud beep. Sean ended the call by softly placing the receiver back on the base. He sat back in the chair with his hand over his mouth. Had they never moved to Blackwood, Vera and Gabe would still be alive and his shoulders held the weight of it every day, since even before *The Great Burn*.

For months before the event, Sean and Vera's relationship began eroding and they both knew it. They argued over petty things, nagged at insignificant, idiosyncratic behaviors, and generally preferred not to be in the same room for too long for fear of upsetting Gabe with their bickering.

The best thing they could have done was up and leave Blackwood and head straight back to New York. They discussed the possibility many times, but Sean couldn't stand the idea of leaving the town without a doctor. The gravity of both situations tore at him so much that he developed a mild ulcer.

Sitting at Talia's desk, Sean remembered a specific fight he and Vera had about six months before *The Great Burn*, one that seared itself into his brain.

Sean arrived home after a hectic day at the office, one in which three people vomited, one in the lobby and two in exam rooms. The flu had taken hold of the town in a springtime bout that forced them to close the grade school for three days. The most severe cases resulted in Sean sending ten people to Albuquerque for brief hospital stays.

Sean reached the kitchen to find Vera yelling at Gabe for him not eating his dinner. The boy had clearly been crying and was now sobbing softly. Normally, Vera was patient but firm with Gabe. That day, her stress levels had gotten the best of her.

Sean was already stressed out himself, so he had no desire for it to continue at home. Without saying a word to either of them, Sean placed his bag on the ground near the doorway to the kitchen and retrieved an open bottle of wine from the fridge and two glasses from the cabinet. He poured both glasses, leaving the bottle on the counter, and walked over to the table where Vera and Gabe were seated. He placed a glass down on the table near his wife and took a seat across from her. His own glass was half empty by the time his butt hit the seat.

Vera looked at wine glass but didn't pick it up. She couldn't decide if it would make the situation better or worse.

Looking back at Gabe and tired of the fight, Vera said, "Fine. Gabe get up from the table and go watch TV in the living room. If you get hungry later, tough shit."

Sean chose not to intervene. Vera appeared ready to snap.

Gabe slid off his seat and ran to the living room. A few seconds later, the TV could be heard flipping from channel to channel until settling on a high energy cartoon.

Vera decided to try the wine, sipping lightly as she stared off into the distance.

Sean finished his glass and just sat back, trying hard to let the tension of his day go.

It wasn't going to work. The wine wasn't going to help. Each with their own negative energy, an argument was bound to occur. Sometimes, as they knew all too well in those days, a fight needed to happen just to release the built-up tension.

They sat in silence until Vera finished her wine, both with a million conversations and emotions running through their minds with neither wanting to be the first to speak.

Vera closed her eyes and found the topic bothering her the most in that moment. "I'm tired," she said, calm and stoic, "and I don't want to be here anymore, Sean. This shitty town, this shitty house," she paused without saying the words she truly wanted that statement to end with. "I'm not happy. And I don't think you are either."

Sean felt insulted by the notion she thought Blackwood and the house were shitty, and he could easily tell where her statement was headed.

"So, why don't you just say it. You have a shitty life, Vera."

"I didn't because it's not entirely true. I have you and I have Gabe, and that should be enough but it's just not. I'm sorry if that reality comes as a shock."

"I just don't feel like you're even trying."

"Jesus, Sean, you can't possibly be that obtuse?"

"You don't have to insult me," Sean snapped back.

Vera rose from her chair. "Apparently, I do." She escalated her tone and volume. "Are all my efforts lost on you? Did I move here? Yes. Did I give up my big city career to be your fucking accountant? Yes. Do I stay at home to take care of Gabe? Yes."

Incredulous, Sean looked away. She wasn't wrong and he knew it.

Vera continued, "YOU needed to do this. YOU felt obligated. But you don't owe these people anything. There's a reason you left and you never should have come back."

Her words from that day stuck with Sean. Vera was right. He never should have returned to Blackwood. Had they not moved, they'd all be in New York - happy, healthy, and more importantly, alive.

The electronic bell above the office door chimed, forcing Sean from his memories. He turned the chair to the right, stood up, and walked around the wall into the lobby to greet whomever had arrived. It was still quite dark so he turned on the lobby lights. As the room illuminated, he expected to see Talia.

When he saw the man that fit the description Toby had conferred to the group about the mysterious agent, Sean stepped right up and offered a hand.

"Agent Learza, I presume," Sean said, confidently but welcoming.

"Doctor Atwater, I presume," Angel retorted, shaking Sean's outstretched hand. "My reputation precedes me."

"Don't think much of it. Small town. Anything new that goes on around here is often known to everyone within about fifteen minutes." Sean smiled. "What can I do for you?"

"I'm here about a patient of yours. Phil Reece. You were one of the last people to see him yesterday, correct?"

"I guess so. After I examined him, Toby took him home and I don't think anyone has seen him since. Then again, we haven't asked around town yet. You know, places he frequents, etcetera."

"Is this unusual behavior for Phil? For his whereabouts to be unknown?"

"Do you know about what we call *The Great Burn*? Happened here about a year ago?"

"I'm aware."

"Well, ol' Phil was found lying in ditch on the edge of town the next day, oblivious to what had happened. Lost all four of his kids. So, in answer to your question, wouldn't be weird at all if we found him right now in that same ditch. Hungover. Maybe dead. Who knows?"

"That's blunt. No sympathy for the man? You two not get along?"

Sean was aware enough in that moment to see the questions had turned to investigatory. From that point forward, he would tread carefully.

"It's not that. It just wouldn't surprise me. He may have suffered some kind of neurological episode yesterday that had me worried. He's supposed to get a more thorough evaluation in Albuquerque. With his history of drinking and a general lack of giving a crap about his health, nothing would surprise me with Phil."

"Fair enough. Well, I won't keep you. This time tomorrow, if you still haven't found him, call me and I'll see what I can do to assist in your efforts." Agent Learza pulled a card from inside his jacket and handed it to Sean.

"Much appreciated." He took the card and without looking at it, placed it in his left pants pocket. "All righty, have a good one then." They shook hands again.

Agent Learza left the office, Sean right behind him to lock the door. He watched the agent through the tinted glass of the door as the man got into his car and drove away, heading in the direction of The Empty Diner.

There was something odd about the man. He couldn't quite put his finger on it, but of the two strange men that had come to town in the last twenty-four hours, Special Agent Learza came off as the more peculiar one. This, of course, was based on a single meeting and with no firsthand experience with the man in black, but nonetheless, the mysteries in Blackwood were mounting.

As he stood there staring out of the window, Sean began analyzing the last twenty-four hours. He couldn't remember the last time anyone new showed up in Blackwood, let alone two such people. He was sure there had to be frequent visitors considering their reluctant fame, he just couldn't recall a specific one in the recent past. On top of that, he couldn't pinpoint the last resident that came into his office with a serious condition, save for Phil the day before.

"I'm way too young for early onset dementia." Sean shook his head. "I'm not blacking out, am I? I mean, Jesus, I've never woken up in a strange place but something is amiss here. I seem to have lost blocks of time. Maybe Talia's right about me needing to see a therapist. Thinking about it, even a vacation might be in order."

Sean rubbed his forehead to relax the tension of a headache that was attempting to settle in. He exhaled loudly.

Ready to take Talia's advice, Sean dumped the coffees down a sink, shut down the office, and set out to leave with the pastries and his bag.

As he walked past Talia's desk this time, something caught his eye that he hadn't noticed before. Right behind her chair, there was a black mark on the gray carpet. Curious, he walked over to it and crouched down to get a better look. With only the low accent lighting on, he couldn't see well enough to make out any details.

He put his bag and the box on the ground nearby and used a flashlight app on his phone to get a better view of the black mark. The concentric circle of black ash was about four inches across and about a quarter of an inch thick. As he brought his face closer, the smell of burning wood wafted upwards. He had no idea what to make of it. The smell brought back a flood of memories from *The Great Burn*, ones he didn't want to entertain, so he grabbed his stuff, sprung back up, and rushed out of the building and to his car.

With the one-year anniversary of *The Great Burn* coming soon, Sean lamented the timing of his fight with Talia and the disappearance of Phil. For the town to have compounding serious issues to deal with might just break their already fragile spirits and sensibilities. If his own emotional state were any indication of what might be happening with others, he understood the next few days were going to be trouble.

Sitting there alone in his car with his mind scrambling, his thoughts went to Vera. She had an uncanny ability to reel Sean in when he suffered from buildups of tension. He didn't always do well in alleviating them on his own. His personality kept him calm and collected under pressure, part of what made him a good doctor, but like most people, his unchecked stress would accumulate.

Vera always knew the right words to say, the right direction to point Sean to get him past the rough spots. Without her, he wasn't entirely sure how he'd get past the current crisis. His mind searched for the next closest thing.

Sharon.

He decided to shoot her a text and see if she wanted to join him for dinner and a drink at his place. While his relationship with Sharon was barely more than an acquaintance, her desire for it to be more was not lost on him. He didn't care about that, not at that moment. He felt vulnerable and needed someone to talk to, someone to help him unwind. He would make his intentions clear with her as he didn't want to lead her on, but what he truly needed was a friend, something he lost when Vera was killed.

He sent a text.

'Hey. If ur not busy tonight, I'll take you up on that lasagna. I'll provide the wine. My place? 7pm? Just in need of friend to talk to. Nothing more. Sean'

Not even a minute passed before Sharon responded.

'Absolutely! I'll be there at 7. Thanks for the invite'

He confirmed her text with a smiley face.

Sean pulled away from his office headed home with the tiniest flicker of hope that the day might not end as poorly as it had started. He needed an adult conversation without conspiracy theories, supernatural leanings, or the unknown whereabouts of the town drunk. Certainly, Sharon could accommodate a return to normalcy, if such a thing existed in Blackwood anymore.

17

Sharon did not want to seem too eager, so after texting Sean she'd be a few minutes late, she arrived with food in hand at fifteen after seven. She wondered what finally made him decide to see her outside of the Food Mart, but it didn't really matter. She was just happy he finally did.

As she stepped to the door, Sean opened it before she could knock. He had been watching through the front window for her to arrive and was full of doubt about inviting her over, but now that she stood before him, he was happy to see her.

"Hello, Sharon." Sean said with a smile. "Let me take that."

She handed him the foil covered baking dish.

"Come on in." Sean moved aside and let her pass. "Make yourself at home." He balanced the pan in one hand and shut the door. Does this need to go in the oven?"

"Just for a bit. Twenty minutes on 400 degrees will do it." Sharon placed her purse on the coffee table.

Sean went to the kitchen, turned on the oven, placed the pan inside on the middle rack, and set the oven timer for twenty minutes. He came back to the living room.

"Can I make you a drink?"

"I'm easy. I'll have whatever you're having."

"Jack and coke tonight."

"Sounds good."

"Go ahead and sit. I'll be right back." Sean returned to the kitchen.

Instead of sitting immediately, Sharon slowly wandered around the living room, checking out her surroundings. The home had clearly been updated. The walls were light gray, the hardwood floors the same, the trim and casings all bright white, and the furniture a mix of navy blue and charcoal gray, all modern but with contemporary sensibilities.

"Makes my place seem like a fuckin' dump," she whispered.

One thing that caught her attention was the massive picture window on the front wall, opposite the couch. The dark gray curtains were drawn tight to either side, leaving a full view of the front yard and the street past that.

She turned toward the front door and noticed a framed picture lying face down on the entry table, so she picked it up. Sean, Vera, and Gabe were in the picture. They looked incredibly happy. The image made her heart hurt. All Sharon knew was that Vera and Gabe were lost to *The Great Burn* but she had no idea where Sean was during that time, what he witnessed, and how he survived. Generally speaking, those kinds of details were not discussed by the surviving residents of Blackwood. Maybe that was part of the reason they all seemed to have such a hard time moving on. She returned it to its originally position.

It had been nearly a year since then and Sean could barely stand to look at a picture of his family. Not that she was surprised but it made it clear to her that Sean was having a difficult time moving on. Sharon was single and lost no one close in the event, so she could only imagine what it might be like to lose both a spouse and a child under such horrific circumstances.

She shook her head and felt a deep sadness for Sean. *If he would open up to me, perhaps I could help ease his pain,* she thought. *And maybe I could find a way to move on too.*

With a drink in each hand, Sean returned to the living room to find Sharon on the far end of the couch. He walked over to her and offered the drink.

She leaned forward and accepted. "Thank you. This place is really cute. I'm guessing it was pretty outdated before you moved in and remodeled it."

Sean took a seat in the recliner instead of the couch so he could more easily she Sharon without twisting. Vera led all the design choices. She had a great sense of style, he remembered. He had no intention, however, of bringing up Vera in a conversation with Sharon. It seemed wrong somehow. He took a sip of his drink before answering.

"Hadn't been redone since the late seventies, if I remember correctly. Lot of mustard color and way too much carpet. Even in the bathrooms."

"That's nasty," Sharon replied. "I never understood carpet in kitchens and bathrooms. Mold and mildew waiting to happen."

Sean nodded. Nervously, he took another sip. After a trying couple of days, he hoped some rational conversation with a friend might be just the ticket to overcome the craziness, but now that he was sitting in his living room with Sharon, he started to think he might have made a mistake. He wasn't entirely sure why. It was just a feeling. *Perhaps unfounded,* he thought.

They sat for a few minutes in silence, drinking. It was a bit odd but not awkward.

"So?" Sharon asked with no idea what to discuss.

"Sorry. I don't really know what to say at this moment."

"That's ok. Nothing wrong with sharing in a peaceful silence. I'm glad you messaged me."

"Yeah, these last couple of days have been ... weird. You know Phil Reece? Runs that auto shop."

"Of course. Why?"

"Apparently, he's missing."

"Oh? Really?"

"Yep. There was some incident at the diner yesterday morning. He got sick and came to see. No one has seen him since."

"Well, we all know he's got a drinking problem. Probably passed out somewhere. He'll turn up."

"I hope so. Odd thing is, this federal agent showed up out of nowhere and talked to Toby outside of Phil's house, and then later came to my office asking questions."

"Huh. What did the agent want?"

"Not much really. He's apparently here in Blackwood for some other reason but just happened upon Toby looking for Phil and asked what was going on. Since I was one of the last people to see Phil, he came to see me. Gave me his business card and told me call if Phil didn't turn up after a day. As of right now, still no Phil."

"It's gonna be tough on people for the next few days with the ... you know." Sharon looked down to her glass and realized she had already finished her drink. "He's been spiraling for years. After the burn, well, it's amazing, quite frankly, that he can function at all."

"True." Internally, Sean debated whether or not he even cared to discuss the topic of *The Great Burn* or its subsequent consequences. He needed to get it off his chest, he understood that. The booze would make it easier. "To be honest, I've had my struggles with all this." He looked away. "I don't know, it's just so hard." He turned back and stood up. Reaching for her glass, he asked, "Can I make you another drink?"

She stood up too and handed over the glass. "Let me come with and check on the food. It's probably nearly done."

"Okay. Go ahead. I'll follow."

Sharon passed by and led them through the formal dining room, glancing around to admire more of the décor and design choices, finally passing through to the kitchen.

They both inhaled the ever-increasing aroma of the lasagna, looking to each other in a shared delight.

"Can't wait to dig in to that," Sean said as he placed the glasses down on the counter to begin prepping another round.

Sharon grabbed the potholders from the counter and used them to remove the pan from the oven. Peeling the foil away, she discovered the cheese on top had melted enough to call the dish done.

"We're good here," Sharon said. "Let's just let it rest five minutes before we cut into it."

Sean had prepped two more drinks and handed a refreshed glass back to Sharon. "So, can I ask you a personal question, one that you may not feel comfortable answering?"

"Sure. I have nothing to hide."

"Why did you come back to Blackwood, and why do you continue to stay here?" Sean put up his hands. "And don't get me wrong, I'm not trying to pry or judge. I'm just curious because I'm trying to understand my own reasons for doing the same, especially the later part."

"It's fine. I've actually thought quite a bit about the whys. I mean, I came back because I needed something familiar and comfortable in my life after a few rough relationships."

"That's as good a reason as any. You lose anybody close in the burn?" Sean took a big gulp of his drink.

"A few friends. Nothing like what you lost, if that's what you're getting at."

Sean nodded. "Yeah, well, I suppose that's my biggest issue. I brought my wife and son here, as you know, to take over for Dr. Mayweather when he passed. Vera wanted nothing to do with it. Leaving New York was a constant strain on our marriage." It felt good for Sean to have spoken those words aloud to another person. He wasn't sure Sharon was the appropriate target for his release, but he needed it. He was beginning to feel vulnerable and thought about stopping. A voice in his head said *fuck it*.

"I should really leave Blackwood and never come back, but," Sean paused, searching his mind for the right words. "I don't know. I just ... deserve to be stuck here. A kind of penance I suppose."

"It's not your fault, Sean. I don't think we are accountable for acts of nature. Could just as easily have happened in New York." Sharon pulled a metal spatula from a ceramic utensils crock near the oven and used it cut the lasagna into eight equal pieces.

Sean walked past Sharon and pulled two large white dinner plates from a nearby upper cabinet, placing them side by side on the counter. He then grabbed two forks from a drawer.

Sharon served up the food. "Sorry, I didn't even think about a veggie side or garlic bread or anything. I usually find the lasagna to be satisfying enough."

"I barely have an appetite on most days anyway, so this will do fine. Can I get you a bottle of water?"

"Sure. Where should be eat? Dining room?" Sharon asked.

"I usually just eat on the couch." Sean took two bottles of water from the refrigerator, placing one on the counter. Before grabbing his plate, he placed the forks on the plates. "There you go."

"Perfect. I like it casual."

Sean followed Sharon back to the living room. They both placed their water bottles on the coffee table and then sat on opposite ends of the couch.

In virtual silence, they ate and drank and just enjoyed the moment of good food, company, and quiet. Those were the most relaxing moments either of them had had in months.

After finishing their meals, they took the dishes into the kitchen, leaving them in the sink to be washed later at Sean's request, and with fresh rum and cokes in hand, they once again went to the living room.

Between sips, Sharon said, "Well, in answer to your original question as to why I stay here after all this shit. I really don't know. Honestly, I don't know where else I would go."

"I'm pretty much in the same boat," Sean said. "This is my hometown and," Sean hesitated, "without Vera and Gabe, New York just wouldn't make sense to me anymore. I suppose this is the punishment I deserve for bringing her here." Looking off in the distance, Sean worked hard to keep his shit together. The booze had his emotions flowing at little too easy for his liking but there wasn't much he could do about it. He somehow managed to keep himself from crying but he rested on the edge.

"I still think you're being too harsh on yourself," Sharon said as she thought about her own regrets and mistakes. She understood the hypocrisy in her words. Not a day went by that she didn't wish she could go back in time and make a few different choices. To some degree, her advice to Sean was meant for her own ears too.

Sean rubbed his eyes. He knew she was right but it did nothing to alleviate his pain and guilt. Part of him, whether he knew it or not, welcomed the self-loathing, the internal struggle. His wife and son were never coming back. He didn't deserve to have peace or be free of the past. That's how he felt.

From nowhere, something moving fast slammed into the front room picture window, leaving a round, red splatter pattern. They both jumped back on the couch.

"What the fuck was that?" Sean shouted. He looked at the window. "Must have been a bird. Big one based on the size of that circle."

Sharon didn't respond. She couldn't. Her gazed remained locked on the window and it brought back an unrelenting flood of memories that she would rather not have experienced but was powerless to avoid. For a second, she thought she saw a man standing outside in the darkness but the shape disappeared just as quickly. Tears fell from the corner of her eyes.

After a few moments without a response from Sharon, Sean looked over to her. He knew instantly something was wrong.

"Sharon?"

She didn't respond and her eyes remained fixed and were now bloodshot. She seemed to be experiencing something similar to what Phil had described.

Sean moved over to her and grabbed her left hand. He put two fingers to her wrist to check her pulse. He counted as he looked at his watch. *Elevated but not crazy,* he thought.

"Sharon, if you can hear me, try to speak."

Once again, she was unresponsive. A few seconds later, she blinked and gasped for air. She put her right hand to her chest like she was in pain. She appeared confused but was at least ambulant.

"What happened?" Sharon asked.

"I have no idea. A bird or something slammed into the window and suddenly you were frozen. Are you having pain in your chest?"

"I was but it's gone now. Did you see anyone out there?"

"Outside? No. Did you?"

"Maybe ... but maybe not. I think my mind is playing tricks on me. Could I have another bottle of water?"

"Of course. Maybe spin around and put your feet up on the couch, relax a bit. I'll be right back."

Sharon gingerly turned and put her feet up as Sean had suggested, leaning back on the throw pillow that sat upright against the arm. The incident, whatever it was, had drained her of energy, and she was having a hard time keeping her eyes open.

Sean returned with a bottle of water, removing the lid before handing it to her.

She took a few shallow sips before a bigger one. The chilled water made her feel better but did nothing for her sudden lack of vigor.

"Thank you. I feel a lot better, I'm just very tired now."

"I'd like to keep an eye on you, so maybe you could stay the night. I am a doctor, ya know." Sean winked.

"I'm actually feeling okay now, but you're probably right. I don't want to be bother though. I don't drink a ton, it's probably just the rum."

"I have a guest room, so it's really no trouble. I'd feel better if I could check in on you. Not like I sleep much anyway. Let me help you up."

Sean offered a hand and helped Sharon off the couch, although she had no real trouble getting up under her own power.

"I'm really okay."

Sean released his hand from hers and they stood face to face, looking each other in the eyes. There was an electricity in the space between them, but they didn't act on the energy.

Sharon smiled and released a sigh. "Thank you for having me over, Sean. It was a nice evening until that weird mess."

"You're welcome. I admit it was a good change of pace. Follow me. I'll take you to the back bedroom."

He led her down the hallway, pointing out the guest bath as they walked. At the guest room, he flipped the light switch and revealed a quaint but elegant room with paint, furnishings, and bedding in various shades of white, gray, and purple. He let Sharon pass.

"Cute bedroom. Nicer than my place for crying out loud."

"Vera had an eye for it. If it were up to me, it'd likely be shit. I'll be down the other end of the long hallway, or probably in the living room for a while. Come find me or holler if you need me."

Sharon walked over and sat of the side of the bed, removing her shoes.

"We'll see you in the morning," Sean said. "You want the light on?"

Sharon shook her head. "Go ahead and turn it off. And thanks again. Goodnight."

Sean turned off the light and closed the door behind him as he left.

He returned to the living room with a bunch of questions, the most pressing of which was: *What the hell is happening in Blackwood?*

He again noticed the splatter left on the front window, so he walked over to get a closer look. The circle was peculiar. It had an almost spider web like shape that would have suggested the glass shattered upon impact but that wasn't the case. The glass remained completely intact.

"Well, this is odd, but somehow not the weirdest thing that I've seen or heard today." Sean shook his head. "Should probably at least try to get some sleep. I can check on Sharon in a couple of hours."

For the first time since *The Great Burn*, Sean drew the curtains on the front window, leaving on the light before heading to bed.

After a rather unusual day, he fell asleep fast, dreaming of a life where he, Vera, and Gabe never left New York. It was the first peaceful dream he could remember having since his family died. Lost in those dreams, he slept through the night, not once checking on Sharon. He would discover in the morning that Sharon had left before he woke, leaving him a note by the coffee pot showing her appreciation and with the hope of repeating their dinner plans again at another time.

18

Inside a car, in the driver's seat and traveling fast down a neighborhood street. Music played loudly on the radio. A song the comatose man didn't recognize. He could smell strawberry bubblegum. He got the distinct impression he was driving but had no control over the vehicle. He had once again been transported to a place and time that was not his own.

A flash of light. Another location. Same town, he gathered, but a different time. Years later based on the cars in the street. Behind the driver's seat of a car again that was not his own. By the looks of it, something terrible had happened. People were running and screaming, garbage and debris flew around and down the street, broken glass could be seen near many vehicles and buildings. The car accelerated.

Back in the first car, the tires squealed as it took a corner too fast, fishtailing a little before straightening out. From nowhere, the car shook as it made impact with an unknown object. The sound of the hood crunching and the windshield shattering left the comatose man sickened. With red splatter surrounding the circular impact spot on the windshield, he quickly understood what the car had hit. The car, however, didn't slow down immediately.

In the second car, the man peered out of the side window wondering what the hell had just happened that would have caused all the chaos. He had never experienced a tornado but imagined this was what it might be like. He turned his gaze back to the windshield just in time to see the car had veered onto the sidewalk. In the blink of an eye, the car collided with a woman kneeling down in front of a baby stroller.

The comatose man became lost in blackness again, the place he spent most of his time. His head and chest hurt, throbbing. Nothing could be done about it. Pain had become a normalized experience. His thoughts then faded into nothing.

19

Sharon plopped down in her office chair after opening The Food Mart still thinking about the strange incident at Sean's house the night before.

Her thought processes spiraled downward as her past regrets became the theme of her day. She ended up fixating on a memory she wished would stay buried. On most days, she managed to keep the horror of *The Great Burn* at bay, but for Sharon, a few moments from that day held eerie similarities to another tragedy she had experienced. She tried desperately to wiggle her way out of the memory by thinking about Sean but her brain would not allow it.

Her mind began to play tricks on her. What sounded like a basketball hitting the glass enclosure of the bullpen made her jump in her seat, only there was no ball. Suddenly, a crimson splatter mark appeared in the center of the panel in front of her, blood dripping furiously from it. Her only thought: *what the fuck?*

Her question, however, was not genuine. She knew exactly what she was looking at. She had seen the exact mark on the hood of her car right before *The Great Burn*. The experience, however, was a mere duplicate of one she had as a teenager which also left a similar mark and pattern on her windshield. Both of the traumatic memories often formed a confusing amalgamation in her mind.

She closed her eyes and rubbed her face with both hands hoping to scrub it away but it didn't work. Throwing her head back, she said, "Get out of my god damn head!" She pressed her index fingers to her temples even harder. Opening her eyes again, she found the blood had disappeared. She wasn't surprised. She understood the image was only in her mind.

A migraine settled in rather quickly. She kept aspirin on her desk, so she snatched up the bottle, taking four pills with four sips from a water bottle.

A shadow passed over the glass of the bullpen. She thought maybe a customer had arrived, so she got up from her chair to have a look but found no one. She searched side to side, craning her neck to peer down some of the aisles, but she was alone in the store. Another shadow crept by out of the corner of her eye. She snapped her head to the right to catch a glimpse but again saw no one.

She walked to the bullpen doorway. The door itself was propped open as always. "Hello?" she called out. She waited for an answer. None came. "Hello? Is anyone there?" A panic set in. The store had never been robbed in her time as manager but she understood there was always a chance of it considering the amount of cash normally kept on hand.

Sharon wondered if the shadows she kept seeing were nothing more than a projection from her own mind, much like the blood on the glass. As she thought more and more about it, she became convinced of it.

What she didn't witness was the stranger seen outside The Empty Cup was standing outside of the grocery store, peering through the window in Sharon's general direction. There was no telling when he had arrived. Like all the others in town that had encountered the man in black, Sharon had a visceral reaction to his presence, despite the fact she had yet to see him.

She returned to her chair and sat hard, frustrated with her own mental state.

"Sharon, you really need to get your shit together," she coached. "Sean is never going to take you seriously if you act like this." She huffed as she looked around the bullpen, shook her head.

Her mind lingered on the bloody memories. The one from when she was a teenager resonated especially deep. She thought about the collision often, the pain eating away at her nearly every day.

During her senior year in high school, Sharon had finally saved up enough money from her after school job at the local video rental store to buy a used car, and she wasted no time doing so. Despite being in high school, her desire for the freedom that would be allowed by having her own car greatly outweighed the crushing pressure to buy clothes and jewelry. It took her ten months to save the one thousand five hundred dollars necessary to get the rather beat up '92 silver Chevrolet Cavalier, that even with more than 150,000 miles, ran well.

On a Spring morning in her junior year, Sharon started her drive to school just before dawn. The clear skies and cold, moist air had left the town blanketed in fog. At first, visibility was barely an issue, but as she got closer to school, a shift occurred so quickly that it left her unable to see even one hundred feet in front of her car. Combined with her inexperience as a driver and a teenage invincibility complex, she sped down the road unaware of the danger ahead.

Four blocks from the campus, she turned right onto Rosewood and sped ahead. Five seconds later, her car shuddered from a direct impact with another student whose head slammed violently on the hood of the car, killing the fifteen-year-old Jason Hemsworth instantly.

With the morning fog, Sharon had unknowingly wandered onto the sidewalk. By the time she realized what had happened and slammed on the brakes, she was already halfway down the block, her classmate dead in the street. As she sat in the car, she helplessly stared at the blood mark on the hood, an image that would forever be emblazoned in her memory.

Alone in the bullpen at the Food Mart, Sharon closed her eyes and wept. She had carried that pain with her for nearly twenty years, often blaming the karma of that day for her less than stellar success in life.

She grabbed a tissue, dabbing the moisture from her face before blowing her nose. She tossed the tissue in a small metal trashcan to her right.

"You never get over it, but it will get easier." Sharon huffed. "That's what the therapists kept telling me. What a load of bull shit that turned out to be. They told to me to forgive myself too. How could I?" She rubbed her face with both hands.

She thought, *I'm just so tired. Days like this, I just want to go to bed and hope I never wake up.* She leaned back in her chair and closed her eyes. *How many years have to go by as I torture myself? I did a horrible thing but it was an accident. One I can't take back. Maybe this self-inflicted punishment isn't fitting the crime anymore.*

Suddenly, the lights in the store flickered and the music playing through the sound system began to decay and distort. From the back of the store and moving toward the entrance, the overhead lights in each aisle popped and turned dark, cascading with each passing second.

For the briefest of moments, she felt alarmed, but soon after, a sense of peace and calm washed over her. As she opened her eyes and leaned forward, a reflection in the glass in front of her made her spin around and jump from the chair.

The man in black stood before her, towering and ominous. He didn't move or speak a word, his face obscured by the shadow of his wide-brimmed hat.

What really caught her attention was the smell of heat wafting from the stranger. Slowly, the man opened his long, black coat, and although Sharon's instincts told her to run away and cry for help, there was no point. There was nowhere for her go, no time to react, and besides that, her fight had disappeared.

20

Sean awoke completely refreshed. Somehow, Sharon's presence in the house allowed him to sleep soundly, dream peacefully. He was worried when he realized he slept through the night without checking on her, and even more so when he went to her room to find her gone.

The note she left helped to calm him down. He still felt bad for not monitoring her during the night. *Not very doctor-like,* he thought. Immediately after reading the note, Sean sent a text to check in on her. She replied and said she was fine and thankful for the food, the booze, the conversation, and the warm bed, and that she hoped to see him again soon. He replied with a thumbs-up.

As he finished his second cup of coffee, he decided to go ahead and text Toby for a Phil update.

'Hey. Any word on Phil?'

'Nope. Looked around a bit yesterday but nothing.'

'Damn. Can you meet me at Phil's house? Maybe text Raelle to see if she and Ted could help out with a search?'

'Sure. When?'

'I can leave right now.'

'Perfect. I'll meet you there in say, 15 min.'

'See you soon.'

Before he left the house, Talia came to mind. He didn't like leaving things so open with her. He felt an in-person apology and conversation were needed. He thought to call her but opted to wait until after the Phil search. He didn't want to be distracted. Speaking with her might lead to a heightened emotional state, and for dealing with the Phil situation, he wanted a clear and calm mind.

21

Ted and Raelle attempted to stay busy but it was of no use. They had no patrons and nothing but the odd man in black and Phil's disappearance on their minds.

Ted could hardly keep himself from continually glancing out of the front windows in hopes of catching a glimpse of the man in black should he return, although, he wasn't sure he really wanted that, not after their physical reactions to his presence.

Raelle, on the other hand, was crawling out of her skin looking for anything to do as a distraction. She had wiped the entire counter and every table in the restaurant three times, and finally after catching her mindless repetitive behavior, threw her washcloth down on the floor and looked to Ted.

"Maybe we should close up for the day, go help look for Phil," Raelle said. "Not like anyone's coming in here."

"That crazy ass drunk is probably lying in an alley somewhere. Puked and pissed out."

"Don't be a dick." Raelle picked up the washcloth and shuffled a few condiment containers back into place.

"Hey, I'd rather waste what little energy I have doing something that matters. He doesn't care. Why should I?"

"Because you're a better person than he is." Raelle knew she was talking to a brick wall. Ted was always cordial around Phil but he made no secret of his disdain for the drinking.

Ted thought about Raelle's words – a better person. *Not really*, he thought. *If she knew what I had done to my own family, my own brother, she'd think of me as poorly as I do Phil. Christ, really, who am I to judge?*

Ted walked over to the fountain soda machine, grabbed a red plastic cup and filled it with ice and cola. When he turned to Raelle, she had bent over to grab some napkins from under the counter. He stopped to admire the shape of her butt in her black work pants. He softly bit his lower lip as he imagined grabbing her ass with both hands, then pulling her close to kiss her. It wasn't the first time he had fantasized about her. They had, in fact, slept together many times in their shared time at The Empty Diner.

After the first time, Raelle made it clear she was not interested in a relationship with him, nor did she want anything to do with being some booty call, as she referred to it. She didn't want to have to quit the job over a failed relationship and she promised to slap the shit out of him if he couldn't keep his libido under control. And Ted knew not to test her. She was without doubt a woman of action.

Two years after their first tryst and about six months before *The Great Burn*, Raelle decided she needed to get laid, so after they closed up the restaurant on a Saturday night, she asked

Ted if he would walk her out to her car. He agreed, not thinking much into it.

Without saying another word to him, Raelle threw herself on Ted, eventually working him into the cramped back seat of her car where they had sex like two teenagers on prom night.

After that night, Ted never once mentioned the rendezvous to Raelle. Playing a little reverse psychology, he hoped his fake aloof attitude would render her helpless in resisting him. It worked well. Ever since that night, whenever Raelle had the urge, she'd show up at Ted's door with a long coat on and nothing underneath and they'd make love. For both of them, it was nothing more than satisfying a primal need. Outside of the sex, they had no shared interests other than the diner and Blackwood. The unspoken arrangement served them both well but that didn't stop either of them from wondering what if. They never had deeper relationship discussions, but after *The Great Burn* and the odd events of recent days, perhaps the time had come.

Raelle turned around and caught Ted deep in thought and clearly looking at her ass. She thought to sass him but his stare continued despite her staring right at him.

"Ted?" she said with concern.

He mumbled a response but his eyes and body remained fixed.

"Oh shit!" Raelle shouted. "Not again."

Ted made eye contact with Raelle. "What? Sorry, I was lost in a memory." He shook his head and took a sip of his cola.

"Well, Jesus H. Christ, Ted! You about gave me a heart attack."

"I think we should talk later," Ted said with a serious tone.

"About what?" She didn't need to ask. She knew exactly what he wanted to discuss. She had the same thoughts from time to time. She just wasn't sure how ready or willing she was to go there, not with all the weird shit going around. *Then again*, she thought, *maybe this is the perfect time.*

"Let's close up and go look for Phil, then we'll talk. Okay?"

Ted nodded, finished his drink with two big gulps, then went to the kitchen to close it all down.

Raelle did her usual closing duties too. When they completed their tasks, they hopped into Raelle's car and made their way to Phil's house to meet Toby and Sean for the search.

The entire car ride over, Ted was lost in the memories of his brother Frank. He loved his brother, and they had a great relationship, but Ted felt lucky his brother never discovered the truth. That didn't stop the guilt.

Five days before The Great Burn

It was 4:45 am on a Thursday. Ted grabbed the keys to the restaurant before heading to the front door. One of the great things about living in the apartment above the restaurant was he never had to drive to work, so he didn't even have a car. It also meant he could wake up a mere fifteen minutes before he needed to arrive.

After leaving and shutting the door behind him, Ted received a phone call from a number he didn't recognize. Against his better judgment, he swiped the screen to answer.

"Hello?"

"We need to talk."

"Regina? Where on Earth are you calling from, and why so early? What's the matter?"

"Burner phone. Look, Ted, I can't do this anymore." Regina said with a hitch of panic and fear in her voice. She had gotten up a full ninety minutes before her husband Frank and the kids would wake up, all under the guise of starting a new

131

jogging routine. She had made her way to the grocery store parking lot, just a few blocks from the diner.

"We haven't done anything together in months and suddenly we've graduated to the level of burner phone? What's gotten into you?" Ted started his walk to the restaurant, fully expecting the conversation to end quickly.

"Just shut up and listen! I have to tell Frank. I can't..."

Ted interrupts her, "Whoa, whoa, whoa, slow down, Reg. What's really going on here?"

"Will you just listen? I'm trying to tell you."

"Okay. Tell me."

"The guilt, Ted. The fuckin' guilt is eating me alive. Whenever I look at Isaiah, all I see is you. I can't live with this secret anymore."

Ted stopped in his tracks just before rounding the corner to the front of the building. "Reg, let's step back a little. Frank and I are brothers. Isaiah looks as much like Frank as he does me."

"You idiot! I don't mean because he looks like you. He's just a reminder of our affair and that you got me pregnant and I kept that from my husband. YOUR brother. How can you even look him in the face and not collapse with guilt?"

"Because we have to, Reg. If Frank found out, it will destroy the family. We've talked about this. That's why we stopped seeing each other some time ago."

A few blocks away from each other and in their respective parking lots, Ted and Regina both paced back and forth.

"It's easier for you," Regina said. "You don't have to see your son every day. You're conveniently removed."

Ted let out a sigh and shook his head. A pit had formed in his stomach. Before the phone call, Ted was certain the situation was under control and would never be an issue. When he finally stopped pacing, he noticed his left hand was

132

trembling. Instantly, he went from being scared to being angry.

"Goddamn it, Reg! Cut the shit! Whatever's come over you today, you need get over it. You're clearly not thinking straight. Divorce ... broken family ... painful split parenting with your kids. Any of that sound fun to you?"

Regina began crying, mostly out of frustration.

Ted decided to let the conversation breathe for a moment. When it sounded as if Regina had calmed down a bit, he continued, "I get what you're saying, I really do. Can you let it cool off for a few days and then maybe we can talk again, try to figure something out? Please, Reg. Please."

Regina put the phone to her chest and looked up to the mostly dark sky and the few lingering stars. "Please, God, I need some guidance here. I'm being torn apart and I don't know what to do. Lord help me."

She put the phone back to her ear. "I don't know how much longer I can hide this but I'll grant you a few days to ponder our next steps. Think hard about all this, Ted. Think about what I'm going through."

"Reg, I know...," then Ted stopped when he heard the beep from the call being ended. He looked at his phone and verified it.

"Shit." He closed his eyes and took in a few deep breaths. He wanted to chunk his phone into the brick wall in front of him but thought better of it.

He continued on to work, thinking of nearly nothing else for four days until the day of *The Great Burn* arrived. On that day, he lost everyone he ever loved.

22

The late morning sun had disappeared behind a system of low-level clouds that spread across the sky in all directions. There would be no rain that day but even the intermittent shade was welcome relief from the searing late summer heat.

Sean and Toby stood outside of Phil's house, next to Sean's silver Lexus which was parked just before the driveway. The two men knew each other, of course, small town, but they weren't close friends by any means. The only other thing they had in common was Phil.

"So," Toby said, deciding to break the increasingly awkward silence, "you think Phil really had a seizure or something?"

"In all honesty, I have no idea what happened to Phil. Even if I did, I couldn't really discuss it with anyone. Doctor, patient confidentiality and all that."

"Oh, I know. I was just wondering what the odds are of him going missing right after having some kind of bizarre brain episode."

"Don't know for sure it was brain, but I'd say as likely to be related as not, knowing his personal history," Sean said matter of fact. He wouldn't sugarcoat his words or his tone with Toby, despite knowing Phil was Toby's boss and best friend, maybe his only friend.

"Hmmm, well, it's been a while since I came by for work and he wasn't here, at least since, ya know, that day." Toby always came to Phil's defense, knowing the man's history with grief and disfunction. "I did send Raelle a text and asked if they could come help look for him. She said they'd be along shortly. Had to close up the diner."

"Great. We can cover a lot more ground that way. While we wait, why don't you take me through the house? At least then we'll have the most obvious place covered."

"I searched it pretty good this morning, but I suppose another set of eyes on it couldn't hurt."

Toby walked to the house with Sean in tow and they entered.

Sean didn't exactly know what to expect when he came through the door, but if he had to imagine what the home of the town drunk looked like, the place hit all the marks. The house was unkempt, outdated, smelled like a dive bar, and had countless empty booze bottles and beer cans strewn throughout.

"The kitchen's at the back, bedrooms and bath down the hall to the right," Toby said as he pointed to the locations.

"Is he usually awake when you get here to pick him up or are you basically his alarm clock?"

"Some of both. Most of the time, he's right there in that recliner, either trying to wake up or waiting to be."

"I'll check the bedrooms first I guess." Sean walked past the towering Toby; his size even more evident in a small room with low ceilings. "Just check around for anything odd."

Toby nodded and began half-heartedly looking around the living room. He tried to imagine what a crime scene investigator might be hunting for in a missing person's case but couldn't pinpoint any specific thing. The place was a mess. To Toby's eyes, there was nothing odd about any of it. Eventually, he worked his way into the kitchen with the same disappointing result.

In Phil's bedroom, Sean drew the curtain on the only window and was met with a face full of dust. He waved the air in front of his face. With his mouth closed, he coughed a few times and managed to hold off a full fit.

Sean glanced around the room for any obvious signs of a struggle, a note, fresh vomit, anything that might lead them down a path to finding Phil. All he got was more mess, more stench, and a desire to look around outdoors.

He searched under the bed and in the closet, then did the same in the other bedrooms. The bathroom was even worse than the rest of the house. The inside of the toilet had several black rings, yellowing water and porcelain, and the sink and tub were no better. He exited quickly before letting his stomach get involved.

Emerging from the bedroom, he headed straight for the kitchen and cast wide eyes at Toby.

"I know," Toby confirmed with a nod.

"I need some fresh air. I take it you didn't find anything new?"

Sean closed his eyes and bent over, hoping not to puke.

"Nothing. We can check out the backyard. There's a shed out there too but I searched it again this morning and didn't find anything."

Sean raised his finger and then opened his eyes. His confusion over what he saw on the ground overpowered his urge to vomit.

About a foot out in front of him on the kitchen floor was a small black circle of ash exactly as he'd found on the floor of Talia's area at the office. It confounded him. To see this once was odd, to find it twice in as many days was a pattern, and he didn't care much for the implications that rolled through his mind.

After a few deep breaths, Sean stood tall. "I gotta go outside." Sean walked through the kitchen and out of the back door. There was a small wooden deck with two steps down to an overgrown yard full of weeds and a few miscellaneous rusty car and truck parts, a worn wood fence that leaned in many places and was missing pickets, and a white, steel shed near the back right corner.

Sean left the deck and stood just in the yard. If he puked, he didn't want to do so on the deck. The clean air made him feel better almost immediately. He could hear that Toby had followed him out.

"You gonna be okay there, doc?"

"I'm fine. This has got to be the weirdest couple of days we've had around here in a long time. Wouldn't you say?"

"Fuck yeah. After months and months of the same ol' boring shit every day, it's like a cloud planted itself over town and rained crazy shit all over us."

"Well, yeah, that's one way of looking at it." Sean thought about how little things had changed in Blackwood. Months and months, day after day, each one like a fallen leaf floating down a stream, riding the current with no control, until finally coming to rest amongst dozens of other leaves near a rock on the shore. A big pile of identical leaves at a dead end. The imagery bothered him.

"That's depressing," Sean whispered.

"Say what?" Toby inquired.

"Nothing. I was just mumbling to myself. What's in the shed?"

"Garden tools, lawnmower that clearly hasn't been used in quite some time, junk mostly."

"I see."

"There was nothing out of the ordinary, there or in the house."

Sean pondered whether he should bring up the ash circle in the kitchen. Certainly, Toby had seen it. Maybe he was just as reluctant to discuss it. He also wondered how much their search would change if he brought up the fact that he had found a similar ring of ash at the office. The idea made him think of Talia.

Growing worried, he pulled his phone from his back right pants pocket and dialed Talia's cell phone number.

Ring.

Ring.

Ring.

Five more, then the outgoing message.

"Hey, Talia. We're over here at Phil's place and about to do a canvas search for him. Apparently, no one has seen him since yesterday. Lot of weird stuff going on around here, so I just wanted to check in with you, make sure you're okay. If you've seen Phil, can you give me a call? Thanks. And, ummm ... I'm sorry about yesterday. I was out of line. So, call me back if you care to. Bye."

Sean's mind drifted toward places he'd rather it not go. He tried to derail it but the train of thought kept hauling ass down the track.

Weird guy shows up in town.

People start getting sick.

Phil disappears.

Talia not answering her phone.

Two odd ash circles in the last known locations of Phil and Talia.

A special agent shows up in town.

Toby may be on to something with his crazy cloud shit storm theory.

Breaking Sean from his trance, Toby asked, "So, what's our next step?"

"I suppose we should head out front and wait for Raelle and Ted," Sean answered with his mind still on Talia. "Then we'll figure out some kind of grid and start the bigger search."

"Sounds good."

They walked back through the house and out of the front door, continuing on to the street. Just as they arrived, Raelle and Ted pulled up, parking behind Toby's truck.

Meeting at the end of the driveway, Raelle spoke up first. "I take it there's been no luck yet?"

Toby shook his head.

"I re-searched the house and the yard," Sean said. "No Phil and no indication of where he might be." He thought again about whether or not he should reveal the ash ring he found at his office and how it looked similar to the one on Phil's kitchen floor. He decided not to. Raelle looked frazzled enough for all of them. He didn't want any part of sending these people into a panic over a potential serial killer loose in Blackwood who's been leaving a signature. The theory was a wild one, despite the mounting evidence. *Of course,* Sean thought, *Talia isn't actually missing. She's probably at home, still pissed off at me, but safe nonetheless.*

"Well, what the hell do we do now?" Ted asked. "Go door-to-door?"

"If we want to do this right, we probably need to set up a search grid and canvas the area, visiting all the spots Phil frequents, which Toby here has said is very few, so that will make it simple enough." Sean found it easy to take charge of the situation. His demeanor was naturally calm, his thinking practical, and being a doctor, most people took him to be intelligent. "Let me grab a notebook from my car." He waved the group to follow him over.

Sean ran over to his vehicle and pulled a white legal pad and blue ink pen from the briefcase sitting on the passenger front seat.

The rest of the group walked toward Sean's car.

"So, what do you guys really think of this F.B.I agent?" Toby asked.

"Not a coincidence, if you ask me," Ted said. "That crazy dude in the black shows up, Phil disappears, then the F.B.I. rolls into to town. Hmmm..."

"I know," Toby said as they arrived at Sean's car. "What are the odds, right?"

Raelle said nothing. She had seen enough true crime shows to know the missing persons situation they found themselves in was likely to turn deadly. In her mind started turning with dreadful thoughts of serial killers, bloody crime scenes, and autopsies.

Sean joined the others, placing the pad of paper on the trunk to begin writing. Everyone gathered around him.

He glanced around the neighborhood, north, south, east, and west, stopping briefly to remember which streets went in each direction. Looking back at the paper, he began sketching out a rectangular grid of crisscrossing lines. The others leaned in to get a good view. In small print, each line got a street name. He drew a few small boxes in key locations. One for each of the buildings they needed to go to that Phil often visited, one being Phil's house. The others were the grocery store, the gas station, the shop Phil owned, and The Empty Diner. It would work out well for the search. Every place they needed to go to was either south or east. They would only need to take a cursory look north and west. Sean shared the idea that if Phil were completely wasted, he wouldn't likely be able to walk more than a few blocks in any direction. They all agreed.

Splitting into two teams, Sean and Toby heading south, Raelle and Ted heading east, each followed their predetermined paths along the streets and houses of Blackwood, searching yards and alleyways, ditches and culverts, even peeking into the backseats of the cars parked along the way.

The streets in town were quiet for a weekday. Eerily so. The sun would periodically emerge from behind a huge cloud, giving brief moments of energy to the search parties, only to be eclipsed a few moments later by another cluster of clouds that only worked to extract their vigor. Despite this, they continued on their paths.

23

Ted and Raelle approached the liquor store Phil often used to buy alcohol but only when it was on sale. Normally, the Food Mart had the best deal for cases of cheap beer and bottles of whiskey. At 10:45 am, the store was dark, still fifteen minutes from opening. They hoped to ask around if anyone had seen Phil the day before but they'd settle for a perimeter search.

"I suppose it's possible he purchased something, couldn't wait to get home to start drinking, and just went around back and started up," Ted said, pointing around to the left of the building where the employee entrance and the dumpster enclosure could be seen from their position. "He might be laying behind that bin back there in a pile of his own piss and vomit."

They walked back to the location, Raelle a little hesitant to look behind the enclosure. "Check back there," Raelle said, ushering Ted in the general direction. She couldn't help but imagine a grisly scene.

"Okay." Ted kicked aside an empty box and jumped back two steps as a rat appeared and scurried away into some brush near the property line of the house next door. He nearly knocked Raelle off her feet. "Fuckin' rodents."

"Gross, Ted." Raelle said as she grabbed onto his arm to keep her balance. A flash of Phil's body popped into her head, slumped over and covered in rats. She let go of Ted's arm and took a few steps back, her breathing intensifying. She closed her eyes for a moment to gather her thoughts but the vision of rats eating Phil appeared again. When she opened her eyes, she noticed her hands were trembling.

Ted lurched forward fully expecting to see more rats. He poked his head around the corner of the dumpster enclosure and was relieved to find nothing at all. No boxes. No rats. No Phil.

"There's nothing back there. Damn it. We're pretty much at the end of the line here."

With the same relief as Ted had felt, Raelle gathered herself and looked behind the enclosure too.

Ted turned and saw that Raelle's skin had grown more white than usual. "Jesus, you okay?" Ted touched her forward to check for a fever. "You're clammy." He grabbed her right hand and found the same.

"I'm ok now. I let my imagination get the best of me."

"Maybe you should sit down somewhere?"

"No, I'll be fine." She looked Ted right in the eyes. "Really."

"Alright then. Well, there's not much else for us to do here."

"Maybe Sean and Toby got lucky?"

"They would have called if they found him, right?" Ted left Raelle's side and quickly walked around the entire perimeter of the enclosure and visually inspected the rear of the building. There was no sign of Phil anywhere. He circled back to Raelle.

"Yeah, I suppose you're right. Is there anywhere else around here you can think of that he might have gone?"

"No idea. I didn't really know the man. Other than Toby, who would?"

"Are we already talking about Phil in the past tense?"

"I didn't mean to."

"I'm just racking my brain trying to figure out what the hell is going on around here. I can't remember the last time anything even remotely odd happened. Now, in a few days, all this shit. It's too much."

She was right and Ted felt the same way, he was just internalizing it, hoping not to add to any panic that might be trying to settle in. His thoughts, however, didn't linger on the stranger, the F.B.I. guy, or on Phil. Ted thought mostly about Frank and Regina and the kids. The fact that they had died and Ted had lived left him with mixed feelings. On one hand, he was relieved the truth would never come out about his relationship with Regina and the resulting child. On the other hand, survivor's guilt often kept him up at night wondering why he deserved to live and they did not. *I'm the asshole here,* he thought. *Frank deserved better. He was an amazing brother, husband, and father, yet he was taken. Then again, being left behind was no gift, was it? I'm here, alone, full of regrets, and with nothing but time to eat myself alive with guilt.* Ted rubbed his head with both hands.

"Let's just go back to the car and go find the guys," Raelle said. "I'm tired and my feet are starting to bother me."

"Okay." Ted took one last look around, then they started walking on the same path they took to get there.

As they walked, Ted ran a few ideas through is head on how to approach the relationship talk with Raelle. He fully expected her to reject the idea, but he hoped for the best. He was beginning to question whether there was really any point in living without some tangible reason to hang on. Raelle could be that thing for Ted. He hoped that maybe, just maybe, he could be that for her too.

"Ya know," Ted started. "One of the few good things in my life these days is you, Raelle."

Playfully, Raelle waved him off. "Oh, stop it."

"I'm serious. We've danced around this for years. We work well together. I mean, hell, why do we keep pretending? Ever since *The Great Burn*," Ted shook his head, "the only time I feel even remotely normal is when I'm around you. At work, out of work, in the bedroom. Doesn't matter. We're partners, and good ones, whether we acknowledge it or not."

They continued to walk and were a block away from Phil's house. Raelle pondered Ted's words but did not respond immediately.

Ted waited anxiously for her response but understood the gravity of what he had suggested, so he let her take all the time she needed to speak.

They reached the car and Raelle went to the driver's side, Ted to the passenger's side. Raelle stopped short of getting in and just looked over to Ted and he looked back. She thought about what he said and internally acknowledged he was right, but a part of her could not push forward with the answer he wanted to hear. She had demons of her own. A past she kept running from. Fears about the future, her own and Blackwood's. With so much doubt, she did not feel equipped to commit to anything, let alone a serious relationship with Ted. She only hoped he could understand her position and not let it ruin what they did have.

"Oh, Ted." She held a long blink then looked at him again. "I like what we have going right now, and I can see expanding on that a little bit, but I just don't think I'm in the right mental space right now to step it up."

"It wouldn't really be any different, would it?" Ted pleaded. "We'd just be less covert and coy about it. Would that be so bad?"

"You're not wrong, there are just things ... things you don't know about me that might surprise you. Not all of it good, Ted."

"Hell, I'm no angel. Whatever happened in the past can stay there as far as I'm concerned. Damn it, Rae!" Ted pounded his fist on the top of the car. "Just be with me. Life is barely worth living right now. With everything that happened ... and is happening. Why can't we just choose a little happiness for once? Answer me that?"

"Ted, I'm just too distracted right now for this conversation. I hear ya, I do. Just give me some time to think it over. Once we find Phil, and this whole thing, whatever it is, blows over, I promise we'll talk deeper about it. Okay?"

Ted looked away in disappointment.

"Okay?" Raelle pushed.

"Okay. Okay. Just please don't blow smoke up my ass."

"Gotcha. Now, let's sit in the air conditioning and wait for Sean and Toby. Maybe they've discovered something useful."

"Roger that."

24

"Quiet around town today, huh?" Toby said as he and Sean walked down the sidewalk.

"'bout normal these days," Sean said. "Ever since ... you know."

"I suppose so."

"Probably be faster if we split up a little. I'll take this side of the street, you over there, then we'll meet up again once we reach the grocery store. Sound good?"

"Makes sense. But hey doc, how are you staying so calm with all this shit? I mean, damn. I don't scare easily but this whole mess even got me on edge."

"I don't know. I'm just trying to be practical and not jump to conclusions." As Sean said it, he thought again about the strange ash circles he discovered. He had concerns, no doubt, but he felt a responsibility to keep levelheaded for the benefit of everyone.

"Honestly, I'm getting pretty worried about Phil." Toby's face told the story. "I don't know man. I just got a bad feeling."

Sean nodded. "It's not looking good, I will acknowledge. But let's exhaust all our options before we let the worst settle in."

"I can do that." Toby turned to the street. "We'll meet up at the end."

"Yep."

Toby went to the house across the street and began his search of each yard.

Sean did the same, and within a few minutes, they had lost sight of each other.

An hour later, Toby emerged from behind the building across the street from the Food Mart to find Sean exiting the store in a minor state of confusion. Toby ran over to him.

"Doc? You okay?" Toby put his hand on Sean's arm. "What's going on in there? Did you find something?"

"I, uh, oh shit." Sean looked around the area, past Toby, trying to gather his thoughts. His once calm and collected demeanor had now turned to fear and concern. Up to that point, Sean had been their anchor, but the look on his face frightened Toby. Something had changed.

"You're freakin' me out! What the hell happened?" Toby took Sean by the shoulders and turned him face to face. "Talk to me." He let go of Sean.

"There's something I didn't tell you guys. I should have, and I'm sorry about that, but I didn't want to scare anyone." Sean started walking back into the store and motioned Toby to follow him. "Come. I have to show you something."

Toby followed. "What the hell is going on?"

Sean kept walking. "I'll show you."

He led Toby into the store and briefly stopped about ten feet inside the store.

"Look around."

Toby did. There was nothing that caught his eye. "And?"

"Nothing odd?"

"Not that I can tell. Come on man. Just tell me what's happening."

"Nothing is happening. That's just it. It's the middle of a Friday and there is literally no one in this store, save for us. No customers, no workers, no one."

"That's crazy. There's gotta be somebody in here."

"There's not. I swear to you. I checked everywhere. It's like everyone vanished. Something weird is happening in Blackwood. Something changed. I can't figure out what, but I don't like what I'm finding."

"I'm confused." Toby shook his head.

"Follow me." Sean led them to Sharon's office. As they walked, he said, "Funny thing is, I can't even remember the last time I saw another person in here besides Sharon, the manager. I've racked my brain trying to recall a single memory of seeing another human being in here recently but I just can't find one."

They arrived at the office.

"You're sounding a little panicked right now, Doc."

"I'm not. Just look." Sean pointed to a spot on the gray carpet right behind the office chair.

Toby stepped past Sean and looked directly at the floor where Sean had pointed. It took him a moment to process what he was staring at. He recognized the circle of ash. There was one on Phil's kitchen floor too. He didn't make much of it at the time, but seeing a second one opened up a lot of questions in his mind.

"What the fuck is that? I saw something like that in Phil's kitchen."

"That's the thing I didn't tell you guys about. I saw that same thing at my office in the area Talia works in. Then, when I saw the one at Phil's, I got a little worried. Now, we have another one."

"What does this mean? I don't get it."

"Phil goes missing. Circle of ash. Can't find Talia. Circle of ash. Sharon is nowhere to be found. 'nother god ... damn ... circle of ash. I don't know what's going on here, but it's looking more and more like that stranger in town may be up to something. Don't you think it's a little odd too that some special agent shows up in town right after some weirdo does and after Phil goes missing?"

"Of course, but what the hell? Are you saying we have some kind of serial killer loose in Blackwood? That's crazy. If it's true, I say we handle this old school. I'll go grab a shotgun and we hunt this fucker down and take him out."

"I don't think vigilante justice is going to help this situation. It might be time to call in reinforcements." Sean pulled the business card of Special Agent Learza from his pants pocket. His concern over Phil's disappearance was at one level, but now that Talia and Sharon were also missing, Sean's personal and mental investment had grown considerably, and with it, his fear. Using his cell phone, he dialed the number on the card. He held the phone to his ear with trembling fingers and a lump in his throat.

There was no ring on the other end before someone answered.

"Hello?"

"Agent Learza?"

"You got him. How can I help you?"

"This is Dr. Sean Atwater, from Blackwood."

"Hey. Is everything ok? Did you ever find Phil?"

"No, we haven't, and that's why I'm calling. It seems there may be something bigger happening here in Blackwood and everyone's getting worried."

"Oh?"

"Two more people have gone missing. My office manager, Talia, and Sharon, the manager of the grocery store."

"When was the last time you saw or heard from either one of them?"

Sean pulled the phone from his ear and put it on speakerphone so Toby could hear the conversation.

"Yesterday afternoon for Talia. This morning for Sharon."

"Well, officially, it's not really a missing persons case until someone hasn't been seen for twenty-four hours."

"What about Phil? He's been missing more than a day?"

"True, but considering his alcoholism and his history, I think we should wait on that."

"Christ, man. Something strange is happening here and we need help. Well, what about if this wasn't just a missing person's case? There were strange ashy marks on the floor in the last known locations of each of these people. We don't know what they mean, but couldn't that warrant a faster response? What the hell should we do?"

"All I can say is, keep looking for your friends. Check around town, make phone calls to anyone else they knew, see if they turn up. If you can't find any of them by tomorrow morning, we'll make it official. That's all I can do right now."

"Damn it! People are missing and that's the best you can do? Never mind then. I guess I'll have to call you back tomorrow."

Done with the conversation, Sean ended the call without waiting for a response, returning the phone and the business card to his pocket.

"Looks like we are on our own for now."

"Let's go back to Phil's house and wait for Raelle and Ted. Maybe they found something."

"God, I hope so. This shit's wearing me out." Sean glanced around the office for any clue as to where Sharon might be but nothing stood out. In his entire life, Sean had never been so unnerved as he was in that moment. In his bones, he could feel his patience and stoic nature slipping away. He was doing his best not to unravel but he doubted he could hold it together much longer.

They walked out of the office together. When they got to the cash registers, Toby took four cold bottles of water from one of the end cap coolers and kept walking out with no thought of paying. Sean gave him a look to signal he did not approve.

"What? There's nobody in here and I'm getting dehydrated. I'm sure the others could use one too. Here." Toby tossed one of the bottles over to Sean, who barely grabbed it in time to keep it from flying past.

Sean looked around. *Toby has a point,* he thought. *Fuck it.*

In true boy scout fashion, however, Sean took a twenty-dollar bill from his wallet and left it inside the cooler, waving it in the air first in sight of any possible security cameras that might be recording.

They started their walk back mostly along the same path they came.

"Can I tell you something? Something I've never told another living soul." Toby was a big man. A tough man. But he had a soft side that rarely showed. With all the chaos surrounding the town that day, he suddenly felt vulnerable and a need to confess. Perhaps his long-ago Catholic upbringing had made a surprise visit. Sean had that effect on people from time to time. Being a doctor and of such a calm demeanor, his patients would often tell him many things, private things, embarrassing things. He had grown accustomed to the behavior.

"Sure," Sean responded. Internally, he begged for Toby not to confess to being a kidnapper or a murder. He wasn't sure he could handle it.

"I don't know how much you know about Phil and his wife and kids. I mean, Phil has come to you before, right? As a patient?"

"He has, yes. If you're referring to the car accident where Hanna died, yes, I know all about it."

"Good. Well," Toby stopped for a moment, trying to piece together the words and having some doubt about sharing. "The accident was my fault, doc." He took in a deep breath and let out a loud exhale.

Sean tried to remember the details of the car accident that took Hanna's life and couldn't recall any part of it that could have involved Toby.

"How is that?" Sean stared straight ahead, trying not to over react to Toby's words.

"The autopsy revealed they had smoked pot while in the car, and that pot was laced with LSD."

"I vaguely remember something like that. What? You give 'em the drugs?" Sean asked almost jokingly before turning slightly toward Toby.

Toby turned to Sean and gave him a look that answered the question with a solemn yes.

"Oh Jesus, Toby. I was just," Sean scrambled for words, shaking his head.

"I didn't actually give them the weed, but I did provide the LSD to the guy who sold Phil the weed. I had no idea he was going to do that and then sell it to people without telling them. No idea." Toby placed both his hands on his head and grabbed his hair, pulling it slightly. "Fuck man. I killed my boss' wife. I killed her." Toby stopped and leaned over as if he might get sick, breathing heavily.

Sean stopped too and placed a hand on his shoulder. "Easy there, bud. Try to calm down. You might be having a little panic attack."

Toby leaned back and took long slow breaths with his eyes closed. "I'm okay." He opened his eyes.

"I take it Phil has no idea?"

Toby shook his head.

"I mean, I can see why you might feel the way you do, but I don't think I would consider that your fault. They shouldn't have been driving while intoxicated, no matter the drug."

"He's told me many times how badly he wished he had died in that car accident too. Hard to hear that all the time and not feel responsible. When he lost Hanna, his life was basically over. His kids lost their father that day too."

"I'm the wrong kind of doctor to be giving you this kind of advice, but you need to tell Phil. Not for Phil, but for you. While I don't think you bear the responsibility you believe you do, but letting something like that hang over you is eventually going to break you down."

They started walking again.

"That's assuming we ever find Phil, right? At this point, I doubt we ever will."

A lump formed in Sean's throat. He held his own feelings of guilt related to the death of his wife Vera and their son Gabe. It bothered him every minute of every day since *The Great Burn*.

At night, when he sat alone at home, Sean longed for Vera's hand and her long fingers to touch his face, to look him in the eyes with that same passion for life and love that she once held during their days in New York. He closed his eyes and briefly imagined her doing just that. The beautiful visual was quickly overtaken by the memory of Vera on the ground cradling Gabe, blood dripping down her face, dread in her eyes.

25

Sean snapped his eyes back open. They were close to Phil's house.

"There's Raelle and Ted," Sean said as he pointed to her car.

"Hey doc, don't tell anyone what I just told you."

"Of course. Just think about what I said. No matter what happens, things will be better in the end if you do."

Raelle and Ted saw the guys coming, so they got out of the car to greet them.

"I'm guessing you guys didn't have any luck either?" Toby asked but he already knew the answer.

Ted shook his head.

"There is something strange going on around here," Raelle said. "It's so quiet, like everyone left town. Did we miss some fire evacuation notice or something?" she asked as she threw her hands up.

"We were kind of wondering the same," Sean said.

Toby offered the bottles of water he swiped from the store to Ted and Raelle. They gratefully accepted and immediately started to drink them.

"Oh, thank you so much." Raelle said in between sips.

"Of course," Toby responded. He looked to Sean. "You want to tell them or you want me to?"

"Tell us what?" Ted asked.

Sean sorted his thoughts and took in a breath before beginning. "There is definitely something amiss here in Blackwood. We don't exactly know what it is yet, but we have reason to believe we could all be in danger. Phil is not the only one missing. I've been unable to get ahold of Talia, and Sharon, the Food Mart manager is missing too."

Raelle covered her mouth.

Ted's eyes grew wide.

"I've tried calling them both but they are not answering their phones, which in my experience, has never happened with either of them."

"Oh, dear god," Raelle said. "What in the hell is going on around here? We need to call someone."

"I did," Sean responded. "I called Special Agent Learza and he basically told me he couldn't officially get involved until they had been missing for twenty-four hours. Without any real evidence of foul play, he won't do a god damn thing until tomorrow."

"Well, that's total bullshit," Ted said. "Phil's been missing longer than that."

"I agree, but there's more," Sean said.

"Oh wonderful," Raelle said.

"When I went to the office this morning, I found something strange near Talia's desk. There was a small circle of ash on the floor, about four inches across. It was odd. I didn't think too much of it until I met Toby at Phil's house. There was a similar circle of ash on the floor in Phil's kitchen too. It was then I started to get the sense there was something wicked at work here."

"I don't understand," Ted said. "Like a burn mark on the floor?"

"No, not really a burn mark, more like if something circular burned just above the floor and the ash suddenly settled down just below. I've never really seen anything quite like it."

"Why would this circle of ash, as you call it, be at both locations?" Ted asked.

"I don't know exactly, but here's the kicker, I discovered a third ash circle in Sharon's office at the grocery store." Sean used his thumb to point behind him. "The store is completely empty. Not a soul anywhere and I can't get ahold of Sharon either. We just had dinner last night and exchanged texts this morning. I'm starting to suspect something more sinister is at work here."

"I knew that man outside the diner was up to no good," Raelle said. "He's picking us off, one by one." Her voice started to sound panicked. "That agent guy is here trying to catch him. I knew it. I knew something was up. I knew it." She looked to Ted. "I knew it."

"I hate to say it," Sean said, "but you might be more right than we'd all care to admit. We shouldn't panic just yet. I think, right now, we're all exhausted. It's been a long day. Perhaps, the best thing we can do is go home for now, rest up, and if Phil, Talia, and Sharon don't turn up by the end of the day, we'll get Agent Learza involved. I don't think there's much more we can do right now."

"How can we protect ourselves?" Raelle asked. "We don't even know what we're up against. If we have a serial killer on the loose, I don't want to be alone."

"You can stay at my place," Ted said. "I have a pistol in my nightstand."

Raelle knew she would take Ted up on his offer but was taken aback by his making this offer publicly. She tried to brush off the implications and casually play it down. "We'll see."

Toby answered, "I got a 12-gauge shotgun ready for that kind of action. I dare this motherfucker to come at me."

"Probably a good idea, Toby," Sean said without hesitation. "Let's all go home, lock our doors. If we hear or see anything out of the ordinary, we'll stay in contact and call Agent Learza if needed. How's that sound?"

They each nodded.

The sun was several hours past peak and night would soon descend upon Blackwood. They all readily accepted the idea of getting off the streets before dark.

Raelle and Ted got in her car and left the area.

At his truck, Toby offered a handshake to Sean. "Thank you for coming out today and helping with the search for Phil."

Sean shook his outstretched hand. "Of course."

"I know how people feel about him. He's a fuckin' drunk who does nothing to take care of himself, but he's not a bad person."

Sean nodded. "I know that. We all deal with our shit in different ways. Some better than others."

"Honestly, I think you're right about this town. Something is ... off. And I don't mean just this last couple of days, but in general, since the burn. I just can't put my finger on it."

"I agree. Hopefully, we'll get some rest tonight, and we'll wake up tomorrow and get some answers from Agent Learza. It's high time he starts telling us the truth of why he's here."

"Definitely."

"All right, man. I'm headed home to try and sleep." Sean knew that was lie. The last thing he wanted to do was close his eyes and stir his mind up with more crazy dreams. "Call me if anything comes up."

"Will do."

Toby pulled away. Sean, however, was not headed home. He thought he'd at least make a trip over to Talia's place. Considering their argument, she might not have answered her phone out of anger. *At least that way I'll know,* he thought.

26

Sean arrived at Talia's house hungry and tired. In his mind, the evidence of foul play around town had already solidified. He didn't expect to find Talia at home, sitting at the kitchen table, having an afternoon coffee. When he got to the door and knocked, he held the tiniest sliver of hope she might answer. She didn't, and so, the hourglass full of dread kept pouring.

A negative energy had enveloped the entire town of Blackwood. Sean thought it ironic that all this was happening on the cusp of the anniversary of *The Great Burn*. "Like we haven't been through enough," he whispered. "I don't really consider myself a man of God, but if there is one and you're listening, we need a lifeline here. The last thread is being pulled and we're unraveling." Sean closed his eyes and took in a deep breath. When he opened them, he pounded on the door. "Talia! It's Sean! If you're in there, please answer the door!" He pounded again, then walked over to the windows.

The curtains were drawn slightly in the middle, so he pressed his face to the glass, cupping his eyes with his hands.

There was no one around. He remembered Talia having a cat. He tried to recall the cat's name. "Something with an F. Freddy, Frankie. That sounds right. Frankie." Through the window, he couldn't see the cat anywhere. He mumbled, "And if she was last at the office, where the hell is her car? It's not here and I don't remember seeing it at the office parking lot. Then again, I wasn't really looking either. Well, I have to get in there and check on the cat, right?"

He went to the door and tried the handle. Locked. He looked down to the mat and wondered. "You never know."

He bent over and pulled the mat aside revealing a single silver house key. After picking up the key and replacing the mat, he used it to unlock the door and enter the house.

There was just enough light to see his way around. Sean glanced around the living room. There was no sign of a struggle and nothing seemed out of the ordinary. Talia," he called out. "If you're in here, it's just me, Sean." He thought for a second about the chances of her having a gun, and he briefly imagined her coming out of the hallway and shooting him. "Yikes."

He searched the entire one-story house for Talia and Frankie but they were nowhere to be found. The house was orderly, clean. Sterile was the word that actually came to his mind.

Once satisfied he wasn't going to get a surprise bullet in the gut, Sean went back to the living room. With his mind wandering, he left the house, got in his car, and started the drive home. As he made his way through the streets of Blackwood, his thoughts turned to Gabe. When it came to his son, and Vera for that matter, he had trouble remembering anything but the conflict, and most of all, the end. He knew there were happy times – Gabe's first steps and words, his first day at school. When Sean closed his eyes, he could not see those moments. He could only see Vera's eyes and hear Gabe's soft whimper as they lie helpless in the front yard just seconds before the fire took them.

In truth, Sean would have taken his own life rather than bear the guilt and regret but he simply lacked the constitution. Whenever he pondered the idea, he ultimately landed on his continued life being some form of punishment that he richly deserved for making Vera come to Blackwood, and to that end, he would be required to endure the pain, the heartache, and the never-ending despair. In some ways, he believed it to be his responsibility to do so.

As he neared the road that would lead him home, Sean paused at the four-way stop, debating whether he really wanted to go home at all. He desired the isolation of home more than anything, and he needed to rest, but he suddenly felt drawn to go straight rather than turn right. A few miles up the road was Crater Lake, the hole formed by the meteor that changed Blackwood forever. That hole filled nearly halfway with rainwater a short time after the impact from a torrential downpour that was often referred to as biblical. The vast majority of the fires burning after the event were snuffed out completely, but for all the lives already lost, it was too late.

Crater Lake became an unwanted symbol of their loss, so the locals rarely ventured there.

For the first time since *The Great Burn*, Sean drove to Crater Lake, compelled by an unknown force he couldn't explain and chose not to resist. He parked on the side of the road, some five hundred feet away from the actual lake, but left the car running.

He cursed the lake, the meteor, the universe for its random chaos and destruction. After screaming and shedding a few tears, he grew tired. As he sat there in his idling car, staring at the sunset, he lost track of time. He leaned back and closed his eyes, breathing at a deliberate pace to calm his nerves. It worked to relax him, so much so, he fell fast asleep within five minutes.

27

The fading light of the sun set over the horizon. The orange and red light cast over the mesa was reminiscent of a landscape on fire, not a way anyone in Blackwood would have cared to describe it but true nonetheless.

After a long and fruitless day of searching for Phil and the revelation they all may be vulnerable to the whims of a serial killer, Raelle and Ted arrived back at The Empty Diner, exhausted both physically and mentally, but mostly the latter. Despite their long day, Ted still held his thoughts of having a talk with Raelle about their relationship and what he hoped might come of it. Even during their canvass of the neighborhood looking for Phil, in his head, Ted kept running over his feelings about Raelle, his past indiscretions, *The Great Burn*, and how suddenly, everything seemed to be coming to a head in his life, for good or ill.

Raelle pulled into a spot near the edge of the building, closest to the stairway up to Ted's place, and put the car in park.

They sat in silence, only the subtle hum of the engine filling the air. They each looked straight ahead, deep in thought, contemplating the day, what lead up to it, and what the next few days might bring and how they could overcome it.

After a few minutes, Ted broke the silence.

"What are we doing here, Raelle?"

"We're locking ourselves in for the night."

"Don't be cute. You know what I mean."

"I know. I'm obviously trying to divert from the conversation we're about to have." Raelle sighed heavily.

"Isn't it long overdue?"

"Not really. I think we're all in highly emotional states right now with everything going on. You're looking for comfort, Ted."

Ted shrugged and then turned slightly to face Raelle. "So, maybe I am. What's wrong with that?"

Raelle softly shook her head and faced Ted. "I'll admit, I've thought about it from time to time, but I'm not going to let all this heightened fear and craziness force me into being with you. If I wasn't all that interested a week ago, why should I be now?"

"Because tragedy makes us take stock in our lives."

"What tragedy? Jesus, Ted! We don't know what happened to Phil. Or Talia, or Sharon for that matter. I'm scared but I'm holding out hope that there is a reasonable explanation for all this. So, let's not jump to conclusions here."

"It's not just Phil and you know it. You know as well as I do what day is coming up."

"Yeah?"

"THAT tragedy lingers. It's on the tip of everyone's tongue, behind the sadness in our eyes and our words. Even almost a year later, that day still informs the entire attitude of this town. We trudge through every day, pretending that we've gotten over it, pretending not to be lonely and scared and tired, but we all are."

"You're not wrong. I just," Raelle paused to gather her thoughts but had trouble coalescing them into words that would make sense to speak aloud. She closed her eyes as a tiny stream of tears fell from their corners.

Ted leaned in, gently placed his hands on her face, using his thumbs to caress the tears away.

It only served to overwhelm her more to feel him. And she did feel him, but not only his touch, his heart. She wept harder as Ted let her rest her head on his left shoulder and chest. He ran his hand across her forehead and through her hair as she released all the pent-up emotion of the last few days, and maybe of the last year. He cried a little too, eventually allowing his head to rest gently on hers.

A few minutes later, they gathered themselves, and finally able to breathe again, sat back up in their seats.

"You ready to go up? Raelle asked. "And do you have anything to drink?"

"Yes, and hell yes."

Raelle turned off the car, they left the vehicle, and walked up to Ted's place.

Once inside, Raelle took a seat on the couch and kicked off her shoes and socks. "My feet are killing me. All that walking around today on concrete." She brought one foot up and started rubbing the arch.

Ted dropped his keys and wallet on the kitchen table and went straight away to the freezer to grab the bottle of vodka he kept nestled up against the stack of ice cube trays, which he took one of as well. From the fridge, he grabbed a half-empty carton of orange juice. After placing the ingredients on the counter, he pulled two squat amber glasses from the cabinet next to the fridge and made two screwdrivers.

Ted joined Raelle on the couch, placing her drink on the table in front of her. "There you go. That should help."

"You think we're safe here?" Raelle picked up the glass and took a sip, then another.

"We should be. The door is locked. There's no other way in. I've got a loaded gun in my nightstand. In fact, let me grab it."

Ted left the room and returned with the all-black handgun encased in a black leather hip holster. He placed it on the coffee table before sitting down on the couch.

Raelle had no idea what brand or caliber the gun was and she didn't care enough to ask. The presence of the weapon gave her the conflicting senses of danger and safety. She trusted that Ted knew how to use it, but more in that it wouldn't be needed anyway.

They sat on separate ends of the couch, drank their alcohol, and just stared straight ahead. They both needed time to process the previous two days, decompress mentally, and rest physically. As the booze flowed through their bodies, the worries started to melt away.

Three drinks and some leftover chicken enchiladas later, five hours had passed in the blink of an eye. In all that time, they didn't speak once of serial killers, Phil, or their relationship status.

"We gotta open the restaurant in less than eight hours," Raelle said, barely able to keep her eyes open. "We should go to bed."

"Yeah, probably a good idea." Ted yawned right after speaking. "Oh, man. Long day. You go ahead and take the bed. I'll sleep out here."

Raelle gave Ted a strange look. "While I appreciate your chivalry, we've had sex in your bed. I think we can manage a few hours of sleep in there together."

"I didn't want to assume. Normally, after ... you know ... you leave."

"True, but we're under extraordinary circumstances here." Thinking about it, Raelle decided to throw Ted a bone on the whole relationship thing. "Might be good to test out what it feels like to sleep in the same bed with you." She held no illusions about what the statement would mean to Ted. She only hoped he wouldn't over react.

Ted used all his power to refrain from smiling. A simple nod was all he offered.

"I'd like to shower first," Raelle said.

"Of course. I'll just clean up the dishes and head to bed, shower in the morning before work."

Raelle looked to Ted. "Hey."

"Yeah," Ted answered.

"Thank you."

"For what?"

"For dinner ... and the drinks ... and for not being afraid to tell me how you feel. I know it wasn't easy, and I know I'm not making it any easier.

Ted rubbed his cheek, unsure what to say. "I think you're drunk and tired. But I appreciate it." Ted waved her off. "Go get cleaned up. We need to sleep. No telling what tomorrow may bring."

Raelle nodded. From nowhere, she approached Ted and kissed him hard and passionately. When she finally pulled away, and without saying another word, she left the room and went to shower, leaving Ted standing in the living room in a daze.

Once Ted was confident Raelle was in the shower, he smiled and bounced his way around the kitchen and living room cleaning up the dinner and the dishes.

As he handwashed the glass pan he had used to reheat the enchiladas, his face wore the delight of his progress with Raelle. Abruptly, his happiness morphed to terror as his right hand, the one holding the sponge, froze in place and began to tremble. The sponge fell into the sink as he remained motionless, unable to pull himself from that state. He wanted desperately to turn around. He could feel a presence. He had no idea where it originated. His upper lip tickled from the blood that dripped from his left nostril but he could do nothing about it. Little droplets fell into the dishwater below, slow at first, but with increasing frequency.

Unbeknownst to Ted, the man in black stood just outside the front door, hovering there but unable to make a move. He needed isolation for his work. Raelle's presence was a complication, one that would force the stranger to return at a more opportune moment. In a trailing vapor of pitch-black fog, the man in black disappeared from the area.

Inside, Ted finally regained his ability to move and his first thought was to protect Raelle. With rushed movements, he grabbed a towel, wiped his upper lip, threw the towel in the trash to hide the evidence, and grabbed the gun from the table.

He pulled it from the holster, released the safety, and searched around the apartment. He found nothing. He kept his ear open to the shower running. As long as the water was going, he had time.

Against his better judgement, Ted opened the front door and took a peek outside. The night was quiet, the only illumination coming from the amber overhead light at the top of the staircase. He pondered whether he should head down to the parking lot to check around but thought better of it. Walking around alone in the dark with a possible serial killer on the loose seemed careless, even with a gun in hand. Plus, if Raelle got out of the shower and found Ted gone, she'd freak out. He didn't want any part of that.

Ted shut the front door and locked it. He went to the bedroom, took off his clothes, and got into bed, although, he had no intentions of actually sleeping. He'd pretend to, as he didn't want to scare Raelle, and the gun would stay at his side.

Ted let out a fake snore as Raelle left the bathroom and got in bed. She did so as softly and quietly as she could.

Exhausted, Raelle fell asleep within minutes.

Ted, on the other hand, stayed awake as long as he could, his eyelids drifting lower and lower with each passing minute. Within an hour, the exhaustion caught him too.

28

Toby had arrived at the trailer park exhausted, fed up, but ready for war. If some psychopath was making his way through town taking people out, Toby wished the man would show his face so he could take matters into his own hands and end the entire thing with a blast from his shotgun.

After taking a shower and cracking open a beer, Toby lit up a cigar and took a seat in his worn-out burgundy recliner, facing the door of his trailer, shotgun in his lap.

As he sat there in silence, his mind couldn't help but wander back to the day of *The Great Burn*. He and his buddy Perry Szczerbiak had planned a fishing and hunting trip for the weekend, so Toby took Friday off work. They had gotten a late start because Toby once again found himself helping Phil get his shit together that morning so he could run the shop. Their original intention was to head out just before dawn but they ended up several hours behind schedule.

He tried hard to shed the memory by literally shaking his head. Finishing his beer helped. He took in a deep breath and exhaled slowly. It felt good to finally have talked to someone about the guilt he held for Hanna's death, however, he wished the conversation could be had with Phil. As the hours ticked by, that scenario grew increasingly unlikely. When he had awoken that morning, he still held hope that Phil would turn up, but after their search and the other peculiarities of the day, that hoped dimmed significantly.

As the sun set further and further, Toby felt his eyes get heavier by the minute. With his beer empty, the nub of his cigar smoldering in the ash tray, and the shotgun resting in his lap, he fell sound asleep.

He opened his eyes at the sound of a rustling outside his trailer door. It was completely dark out and he wasn't expecting any company, but the trailer park had issues with racoons and feral cats, so strange noises weren't normally something to get worked up about. The events of the last few days, however, made every noise a suspicious one.

From nowhere, a fierce wind blew the trailer door open, causing Toby to jump to his feet, the shotgun falling from his thighs to the floor as he rose.

From across the yard and the road, the man in black stood motionless, his gaze seemingly locked on Toby. While the wind blew leaves and trash about, the stranger appeared completely unaffected by it. The brim of his hat and his long, black coat remained still.

In his brain, Toby sent the signal to bend down and grab the shotgun off the ground, but his body did not comply. Like everyone else in Blackwood that had a run in with the stranger, Toby could do nothing but stare at the man and wonder what the hell was happening.

Suddenly, the world around Toby appeared to tumble, spiraling around him in a terrible case of vertigo. His own body remained fixed. When the spinning stopped, the man in black was gone, the wind had died down, and the vertigo had left Toby nauseous. As the contents of his stomach rose up his esophagus, he quickly turned to the left, finally vomiting onto the floor.

Shifting slightly back to the right, he flopped back down into his recliner, trying desperately to understand what had just happened. He could find no words or explanations, only an unexpected sense of finality, like a task had been completed and he could finally relax.

After gathering himself, he went to the kitchen, stepping over the gun, and rinsed his mouth out in the sink. He splashed a little water on his face too and left it to air dry. His mind once again went to the morning of *The Great Burn*.

He remembered driving toward the countryside in his truck with Perry in the passenger seat. They had a favorite spot they liked to hunt a few miles past a small farm. When they reached the edge of town, the airburst from the meteor passing overhead forced the truck off the side of the road. He remembered Perry asking him – 'What the hell was that?'

A few moments later, a massive rumble popped the truck off the ground like it weighed nothing, and in a flash, his mind went blank. Toby had no other memory past that until he awoke sometime later at home with no idea how he got there, the fate of his friend, or that of the town of Blackwood.

Unbeknownst to Toby, the impact occurred just over a mile past their location in the place now known as Crater Lake. For reasons he couldn't explain, Toby felt compelled to return to that location. So, off he went on foot, out of his trailer, and in the direction of Crater Lake. In a bit of a trance, he took nothing with him. Not his keys. Not his cell phone. Not his shotgun.

In the dark and on the side of the road, Toby walked for miles with little awareness of his surroundings or the man following him the entire time.

29

The comatose man stood in the darkness. Nothing was visible. For no reason, he felt the sensation of his head moving from side to side in a circular motion. Spinning and spinning his mind went for an unknown amount of time until finally it stopped. His stomach ached but nothing happened.

The back of a brutish man appeared before him, walking away. The comatose man followed at the same rate of speed. The only light shone from a few street lights that appeared from time to time.

The man walking ahead of him suddenly stopped, turned around, locked eyes with the comatose man, waited for a few seconds, then vigorously shook his head and shooed him away with his left hand.

The comatose man instantly flew backwards and became lost in the darkness again.

30

When Sean awoke, the sun had fully set, the dark of evening bringing with it much cooler temperatures and a mist across the mesa and the lake. He felt better having slept a little, but sitting near the crater, alone, he was only reminded of what he lost and how he longed to have Vera and Gabe back, or to join them in whatever afterlife may exist.

Noticing the car was still running, he was surprised he hadn't run out of gas. The meter on the dash showed he had an eighth of a tank left.

Looking out of the windshield, the mist was heaviest over the water and patchy where he was and around the perimeter. Many ideas ran through his head as he sat there in the dark.

I could easily just drive right into the lake.

And that'd be that.

Would anyone even care?

Do I care?

I can't even see a future where my life is happy.

Or where I matter.

I miss my wife.

And my son.

I don't want to do this anymore.

The engine of his car roared to life as he unconsciously pressed the gas pedal down. When he finally realized what he was doing, he thought to stop but didn't. He let the power of his emotions take over his actions.

Sean slammed the car into DRIVE and he was thrust back against the seat as the vehicle took off, wheels spinning, dust flying. He steered himself back into the road, the rear of his car fishtailing a bit before it gripped the asphalt.

His headlights were off and there were no street lights, so the only illumination came from a barely surfacing moon. The distance to the water closed quickly. Out of the corner of his eye, he saw something move to his left. Trying to figure out what he saw, he lost track of the road ahead of him. A second later, he realized the moving object was a person, and a tall one at that. Sean could think of nothing but the man in black described by the others. Whomever it was, he was headed right for the water to the same place in the lake Sean was bound to enter.

Time appeared to slow for Sean. Another moment later, Sean determined the person was in fact Toby McNamee. He didn't seem okay. He walked toward the water in a zombie-like state, seemingly unaware of his surroundings. What really scared Sean though was the shadow behind Toby. Without being certain, Sean believed he could see the shape of another man close behind but the details of this person were lost in the darkness.

Sean slammed on his brakes and attempted to turn the car away to the right to avoid a collision. The water came closer as the car spun forward. He braced himself on the steering wheel and closed his eyes so he wouldn't have to witness any impact.

His body jerked violently forward as the car stopped its spin. He released his grip and his head hit the steering wheel, knocking him unconscious.

Surrounded by dark, murky water, Sean floated near the bottom of the lake, on his back, looking toward the moonlit surface. His car was nowhere to be found. As far as he knew, he wasn't drowning and he wasn't dead. And there seemed to be no reason to panic. The stillness actually calmed him. For the first time in as long as Sean could remember, his mind was quiet and he felt at peace. There were no missing people to deal with, no stranger in town to avoid, no burn to run from. The silence of the lake bottom became his mind, the buoyancy his body, the solace his soul.

An unknown amount of time passed for Sean. He closed his eyes and drifted, yet didn't really move at all.

At some point, his body convulsed, bringing him out of his state of bliss and back into the world. He opened his eyes when he heard a muffled voice from above. In the pale light of the moon, Sean could see a small figure at the surface. He instantly recognized the shape as his son, Gabe.

He cried out for him but the sound was lost in the water.

The voice from above came again. He thought he heard the word DADDY.

Sean used his arms to begin the ascension. Using the small cone of light coming from above to guide him, he swam. Higher and higher he went, slowly closing the space until he finally broke the surface of the water only to be brought right back to the reality of life and pain. There was no Gabe, only the dark. He gasped for air, then fell back, floating on the surface for a moment just before blacking out again.

31

The TV in Room 45 had been left on a classic movie channel showing a day-long marathon of Hitchcock movies. Vertigo, starring James Stewart as Scottie and Kim Novak as Madeleine, was playing. In the scene, John "Scottie" Ferguson sees Madeleine for the first time at the upscale Ernie's Restaurant after her husband Gavin hired Scottie to tail her. Gavin suspects she may be possessed.

In the mind of the comatose man, another scene played out. A different man and a woman arrived to the parking lot of a diner, one that felt familiar to him. He watched them from across the street, from the shadows, from over one hundred feet way. He was uneasy about watching them.

On the TV, Scottie is watching a house. Madeleine comes out and gets into her car and leaves. Scottie follows.

The comatose man witnessed the woman and the man parked at the diner get out of the car and head around to the side of the building and go up the stairs. Once they entered the building, his perspective instantly changed. He was no longer hiding across the street, instead he stood at the base of the stairs looking up at the door.

A flash. He stood at a door but didn't enter. Anticipation and fear filled his gut. He had no idea his nose had started bleeding. The medical staff would discover it later.

Suddenly, everything went black and the comatose man drifted back into the abyss of his never-ending cycle of darkness. How long he would spend there was unknown. The man had lost all sense of time. He simply drifted along, his mind active at times, completely gone in others.

32

At 4 a.m., Raelle's phone alarm pulsed to life with the gentle sounds of nature, loud enough to wake her but not Ted. She silenced the phone and went to the bathroom to get ready for work trying hard not to disturb him. She wanted to let him sleep in for a change. At least for a while. Normally, Ted arrived at work around 4 a.m. with Raelle rolling in around 4:30.

They ran the restaurant together. Ted owned it, as a matter of record, managed the operation, and ran the backend, while Raelle handled the front end. In practice, they were partners in the endeavor, both capable of handling any aspect of the business.

Raelle stood in front of the bathroom mirror, trying to use Ted's comb to do something with her long hair. The process soon grew tedious. Before long, she gave up and pulled her hair up into a ponytail using an elastic tie she kept in her pocket.

She grabbed her clothes off the hook on the back of the door and got dressed. She mumbled at the idea of putting on the same dirty work clothes she wore the day before, but without going all the way home to get a clean outfit, she didn't have much of a choice.

She went back to the mirror to get one last look at her hair and her lack of fresh makeup. As she stared in the mirror, she treaded lightly in the previous day's events, instead choosing to focus on the day ahead, one she hoped would yield positive results. Looking past her own image, she caught a glimpse of the tub and shower combination behind her, sending a flash of a memory into her head.

A tub full of dirty water.

Raelle kneeling beside the tub with her hands submerged in the water.

Her mother Sue's lifeless face staring back at her.

Raelle shook her head and turned away.

"No," she whispered. "We're not going to start the day with that shit."

Something Ted had said the day before came to mind. This idea of taking stock in your life. "Well, maybe I don't want to do that," she whispered. *Do I like where my life is right now? Not exactly, but I sure as hell don't wanna go rooting around in the past trying to reconcile my choices. I don't need to. She's better off and so am I. Besides, I live every day with it hanging over me and I'm fine.*

She rubbed her face, covering her mouth. She knew the words were a lie. She longed for the ability to tell someone, anyone, what she had done, to get forgiveness for her actions, to find some kind of peace from the guilt. Deep down, she knew her crass attitude toward her mother's death was a façade, but the coping mechanism worked, at least it had for the few years since then, but as Ted suggested, challenging times in life often lead to a reevaluation of paths. She didn't want to admit it, but she knew he was right.

Tired of lingering in her thoughts, Raelle turned off the bathroom light and opened the door. With soft steps, she returned to the living room, put her shoes and socks on, grabbed her purse, and left the apartment.

The predawn air was dry and chilly. Raelle shivered as she walked down the stairs and as she fumbled with her keys while opening the door to the diner. As she pushed the door open, she got the distinct impression someone was nearby. She let go of the door and took a glance around behind her. There was no one she could see but it left her feeling uneasy. She quickly entered the restaurant, locked the door, and turned on all of the lights. Her pre-opening routine would keep her distracted for a while, so she didn't think much about it again.

Her instincts, however, were right. Someone was watching, just not her. The man in black had returned, fixated on the stairs up to Ted's place. So, while Raelle turned on all the kitchen equipment, brewed the coffee, made the egg wash, and diced the fruit and vegetables, the stranger made his way to the front door of Ted's apartment.

Raelle walked through the swinging door to the kitchen, a sharp knife in her hand, ready to dice the green peppers and onions for the Denver omelets.

The man in black entered Ted's place, not by opening the front door but rather by just appearing on the other side out of thin air. He held no weapons.

After scraping all the veggies into their appropriate storage containers, Raelle stood for a moment and looked around the kitchen, trying to remember all the tasks that needed to be completed. She had set four dozen eggs on the counter that needed cracking, so she continued on to that task.

The stranger had eyes on the bedroom door. There was no need to look around the apartment. Somehow, he knew exactly where his target was. Ted laid fast asleep on the bed, the gun he once held had fallen to the floor.

Raelle finished all the back-end food prep and returned to the front. Desperately needing some caffeine, she stood in front of the coffee machine waiting for the drip to finish. The smell and sound mesmerized her.

Hovering at the end of the bed, the man in black made no sound, made no movement. He simply watched Ted. A minute or so passed and Ted finally awoke. Startled by the shadowy figure standing at the end of the bed, he sat up and pushed himself against the headboard.

Raelle sipped on her coffee, two cream and two sugar, as she stood behind the bar, looking out of the front windows. The street was still dark, save for two streetlights, one of which flickered like it was on the verge of going out. She turned and saw the clock above the service window. 4:48. If Ted didn't come down soon, she'd have to call up there to wake him up.

Ted wanted to speak but couldn't move his lips, or anything else for that matter. Even his eyelids were locked open. Ted thought about the gun he had with him when he got into bed, knowing he had lost hold of it as he slept, but there was nothing he could do to secure it. *I'm trapped,* was all he could think.

To make sure the griddle was warming up, Raelle wet the tip of her middle finger under the sink and quickly pressed it to the flattop. "Shit, that's hot." She backed the temperature knob a hair then looked around Ted's station to make sure everything was in order. Satisfied, she returned to the front line to check the time again.

Unable to vocalize, Ted internally asked questions of the man in black. He was surprised to get answers. At first, he thought maybe he had simply answered the questions himself, but inside, he just knew that wasn't the case. Somehow, he and the stranger were speaking telepathically.

Why are you doing this?

It's time.

The voice was menacing in its lack of origin and ethereal quality, yet comforting too, for reasons Ted could not quantify. The conflicting aspects of it sent chills down his spine and raised the hair on his arms.

Time for what?

For the suffering to end.

Ted thought about those words. He had suffered. The whole town had suffered. For a year since *The Great Burn* and for some time before that, each day came and went with little fanfare, little joy, little meaning. The daily trudge had become a punishment for whatever past deeds they had endured in their minds, whatever sentiments were allowed to linger.

What right do you have to be the arbitrator of that?

I am the only one who can.

That statement confused Ted. This man had no idea who any of the people of Blackwood were and what they'd been through. Or maybe, Ted wondered, there was more to this stranger. Maybe, he was no stranger at all.

Who are you, really?

The answer did not come to Ted immediately. Instead, a glowing ember of orange and yellow appeared from inside the stranger's coat. The fiery light increased in intensity until the shadows could no longer hold and the flame burst from under the long trench coat of the man in black. As the wave of heat engulfed the room, Ted heard the answer to his question. The words comforted him. He even smiled. He closed his eyes and accepted his fate. In truth, the second he woke up to find the man in his bedroom, he understood the time had come for him to go and there was nothing he could do to change it.

Ted disappeared from the room, and the man in black with him. The only evidence of their encounter was a small ring of ash on the white sheets where Ted had been sitting just moments before.

From nowhere, a pit formed in Raelle's stomach. There was enough pain to force her to place a hand on her belly and bend over. The searing ache reminded her of the time she had gallstones but she knew it couldn't be that. For one thing, it wasn't in the right place, and for another, she no longer had a gallbladder. With the pain, however, came the distinct impression something was amiss, not with her, but somewhere else. She thought of Ted and looked to the clock to find it was just after 5. Hobbling to the phone by the cash register, Raelle picked up the receiver and dialed Ted's number.

It rang eight times before going to his voice mail. Using her cell, she sent him a text. 'Wake ur ass up and get to work'.

She waited two minutes for a response, then dialed him again. Still no answer.

"God damn it, Ted. You better be in the shower."

She wasn't willing to wait another minute to find out. Still in some pain, she held pressure on her stomach and ran out of the restaurant, around the building, and up the stairs to the apartment.

She had left the door unlocked so she swiftly entered the apartment to find it as dark as when she left. She turned on the living room lamp and made her way to the bedroom. She used her index finger to gently push the door open. She needed Ted to get up and come to work but she didn't want to startle him.

When she saw the lump on his side of the bed, she actually felt a little guilty about needing to wake him up. The quiet and stillness of the room brought her a sense of peace and more than anything, she wanted that for Ted.

Unfortunately, he had to get up and come to work, so, with some reluctance, Raelle walked over to the bathroom and turned on that room's light. It would be much less harsh than turning on the overhead bedroom one.

"Ted. You gotta get up now." She watched for any movement from him but none came. "Ted?"

She walked to the corner of the bed and detected the slightest hint of a burning smell, like someone had struck a match a minute before. Ignoring the odor, Raelle pressed down hard twice in quick succession on the corner of the bed, hoping to jostle Ted, but there was still no movement.

As she studied the bedding and the spot where she believed Ted was asleep, she began to understand, in fact, that Ted was not in the bed at all. She ran around to his side of the bed and threw the blankets aside, revealing the small ash circle. The fitted sheet beneath it had charred but not enough to burn through.

Her eyes widened and a look of sheer terror drew across her face, sending her skin to a shade of white way beyond pale. At first, she couldn't move, and maybe she just didn't want to. She shifted her left foot and discovered the gun on the floor. She bent down and picked it up, putting it to her nose to see if had been fired. It had not. Confused and with the adrenaline built up, she bolted around the apartment in a state of panic in search of Ted, the gun out in front of her. After checking every closet, in every corner, in every room, she fled from the apartment and down the stairs.

33

When Raelle reached the parking lot, she was stunned and pleased to discover Sean's car parked right in front of the diner. She wondered how long he had been there, perhaps was even a bit curious as to the timing of his arrival. Regardless, she was glad to not be completely alone.

Barely able to hold onto the gun with her shaking and twitchy hands, Raelle ran to the driver's side of Sean's car and tapped on the glass with the butt of the gun.

Sean appeared to be asleep but snapped awake at the clacking noise to his left. Looking out of the windshield, he recognized the diner but had no clue as to how he had arrived there. Trying to jog his memory, he could recall being at Crater Lake but not much else. Another firm rap at the window drew his attention to his left.

He shrugged sideways in his seat out of fear when he saw the gun. Even more surprising to him was that Raelle was on the other end of it.

She motioned for him to roll his window down.

Sean put his hands up with his fingers spread then slowly lowered his left hand down to the door to press the window button.

"Raelle? What's going on?"

"It's Ted. I can't find Ted."

"Can you lower the weapon please? What are you doing with that thing?"

"Oh, sorry," Raelle said, nearly out of breath. She looked to the gun and realized she was being a little too casual with where she had been pointing it. She put her arm down and stepped back.

Sean rolled up the window and got out of the car. "What happened?"

In a frantic state, she said, "I have no idea. I stayed at Ted's last night, and I got up a little early to open the restaurant and let Ted sleep in. I tried to call him to wake him up and when he didn't answer, I went upstairs to get him and he was gone. But Jesus, Sean." She shook her head.

"What?" Sean asked with high anticipation.

"There was an ash circle on the bed. A god ... damn ... ash ring, right where Ted was sleeping. And now he's gone. What the fuck is going on, Sean?" Raelle started to cry. She covered her eyes with her free hand and tried to gather herself.

Sean bit his thumb nail, no longer able to hide his worry. "I really don't know, but I think it's time to call in the Feds." Sean took his phone from his right pants pocket and used the call history to dial Agent Learza.

The phone rang and rang but no one answered and there was no outgoing message and no beep. Sean ended the phone call and shook his head.

"No answer."

"Well, it is five in the morning. Maybe he's still sleeping or in the shower or something."

"I suppose so. What about the sheriff's office?" Sean went into his contacts and was surprised to discover there were only a few numbers. "Hmmm, that's weird. I was pretty sure I had the number in my phone."

"Dial 9-1-1."

"Ok." Sean did exactly as Raelle suggested but got the same result as when he tried Agent Learza.

"God damn it!" Sean barked. "What the fuck is going on around here. Since when does the emergency number go down?"

"I don't like this, Sean." Raelle caught sight of the eastern horizon. The sunlight had crept high enough to create a glow but what bothered her more was the growing dark clouds that rose just above that horizon.

Sean saw Raelle staring off into the distance. "What is it?"

"Not sure. Those clouds. They seem to be spreading quickly and are headed straight for town. It might pour soon."

To Sean's eyes, the formation didn't look at all like clouds, more like thick, charcoal gray smoke.

"I don't think those are clouds." He paused for a moment, as he really didn't want to say what he truly thought it was, but he knew he had to. "Is there a wildfire nearby? Because I'm pretty sure that's smoke."

Raelle sighed and shook her head. At a stress breaking point, she chose not to even dive into the possible implications, especially considering the amount of stuff they were already dealing with.

"I can't even ... not right now," Raelle waved off in the direction of the smoke. "I'm worried, Sean. We need to find Ted, and Phil, and the others. I'm going to tear my hair out if we don't figure something out soon."

"I know. We need to keep it together though." Sean closed his eyes and rubbed his face and head with both hands. He believed what he had just said to Raelle, but what he really wanted to do was scream, drink a bottle of whiskey, fall asleep, and forgot about everything.

"We should check on Toby," Raelle said.

"Great idea. You know where he lives?"

"Rocky Point Trailer Park. Last one on the left off the main road." Raelle looked to the restaurant. "Shit. I need to go turn off all the kitchen stuff before we go. We sure as hell don't need anything burning down right now."

"No. No we don't. You got any coffee on yet?"

"Oh yeah. I'll grab you one. Be right back."

Raelle returned to the diner.

Sean turned back to the horizon and worried about the smoke. Even though it looked nothing like the encroaching groundburst of *The Great Burn*, it reminded him of that horror nonetheless. The mass of black moved swiftly, so much so, it appeared unnatural. By his best estimation, Sean believed it would hit town within the hour. Whatever they were going to do, they needed to act fast. They wouldn't want to be outside when it arrived, not without a mask.

As he waited for Raelle to return, he pondered the last few days. He could clearly remember waking up and skipping his usual run to the diner because he missed his alarm. He remembered Phil coming in to see him at the office, and shortly thereafter, pissing off Talia. There was a chat with Sharon that day before he went home. The next morning, he recalled making it to The Empty Diner and having a conversation about a stranger in town and how Phil was missing. He remembered meeting Special Agent Learza, reading Talia's note, his dinner with Sharon, the fruitless search for Phil, and the growing concern that someone, perhaps this man in black, had laid siege on their quiet town and was playing some sick game on the eve of the anniversary of *The Great Burn*. There was also a brief memory of being parked at Crater Lake, and then suddenly and without explanation, waking up in the parking lot of the diner with a gun pointed at him. *Not your typical day in Blackwood,* he jokingly thought, a lighthearted moment at a time when the tension and dread had swelled beyond all reckoning.

Sean closed his eyes and searched hard for a pleasant memory, one that involved Vera and Gabe. He settled on the details of a Saturday afternoon a few years before his family moved to Blackwood.

It was Gabe's second birthday. Vera's parents had driven down from Vermont. They worked hard to be present at their grandson's important life moments. Vera was their only child and Gabe their only grandchild, so they took special delight in them.

The best part of the day was placing Gabe in his highchair and putting that plate in front of him with the vanilla cake and blue icing. He wore only a diaper as they knew the mess he would make eating that cake with his bare hands. By the end, they guessed Gabe had actually eaten less than half the piece of cake, with the vast majority of it spread in some manner on the highchair tray, the floor, and the boy's chest, shoulder's, belly, face, ears, and hair. They all laughed so hard their bellies and cheeks hurt as they took pictures and videos of Gabe smiling and giggling his way through the cake. Vera could be heard saying that Gabe looked like he devoured a Smurf.

The memory brought a tear to Sean's eye, leaving a single stream rolling down his cheek. His lips quivered. He longed for days like that. He didn't want to open his eyes for fear of returning to his new reality. He leaned back against the car and slid down to the ground and onto his rear. He fought back the flood waiting to happen, worried Raelle would unravel if she saw that he couldn't keep his shit together.

When she emerged from the diner, Sean jumped to his feet, brushing the dirt from the back of his pants.

"You okay?" Raelle asked. She had two disposable cups with coffee in her hands. She handed one to Sean.

He accepted. "Thank you. I'm fine. I was just ... it's nothing." As discretely as he could, he used his free hand to wipe the moisture from his cheek. "We should go see Toby. Let him know about Ted. Plus, we don't want to be out when that smoke gets here."

"Definitely," Raelle responded. "Your car or mine?"

"Mine's fine."

They entered the vehicle and took off for Toby's trailer park. Sean knew exactly where it was, being the only one in town, although he was fairly certain he had only ever passed by it a few times and had never once pulled in.

They had sat in silence until about halfway there when Raelle spoke up.

"I have a really bad feeling about all this, Sean. I've never spoken to anyone about his before, but fuck it. With all this shit going on, there really isn't much to lose."

"What is it?"

"You know, ever since *The Great Burn*, this town, the people in it, life in general, has seemed ... off. Like right now. Look around. Look at the streets."

"Yeah?"

195

"Where is everybody? There's literally not one person around ... anywhere. Like the grocery store or the diner. Where the fuck did everybody go?"

"I was wondering that yesterday. Town seems abandoned. I don't know. I guess before recently, I never really thought about it. But yeah, it's been that way, like you said, since *The Great Burn.*"

"Exactly. Glad I'm not the only one who noticed. It's almost as if the town exists in a snow globe or something, and every once in a while, someone comes along and shakes the damn thing and the snow blows around. Or in our case, the dust."

Sean thought about her words and couldn't argue against it. "You're right. It's like we've been sitting on a fireplace mantle, nothing going on at all until suddenly someone comes along and shakes our little world. That's messed up but a great analogy."

"Another thing too," Raelle said.

"Oh?"

"When was the last time you went anywhere?"

"How do you mean?"

"I mean, like, out of Blackwood. When I was at Ted's last night taking a shower, I was racking my brain trying to remember the last time I went anywhere that was not in the city limits. Couldn't think of a single instance. Not one. You?"

Again, Sean searched his, as of late, flawed memory, and like Raelle, could not come up with even one example of having left Blackwood since *The Great Burn.*

"Honestly, I got nothing."

"That's the kind of shit that's really freaking me out. I don't really even know where I am right now. I mean, this looks like Blackwood. Smells like it. You seem real enough. The Matrix is what comes to mind."

Sean didn't respond. He got the sense from Raelle's tone of voice that she was nearing the end of a very short rope of sanity. He feared that once it became too frayed, she'd spiral out of control.

He turned onto the long drive of the trailer park. Nothing seemed odd except for the obvious lack of activity. The entire place was eerily devoid of people. There weren't even any dogs barking, which especially caught Sean's attention. He could not recall the last time he even saw or heard a cat or dog in town. Other wild life, yes, like a few birds and rodents, but no domestic animals. Even Talia's cat was nowhere to be found. In fact, there were no farm animals either.

The road continued on for a minute to the edge of the property where they finally saw Toby's truck. Sean pulled in right behind, put the car in park, turned it off, and they exited the vehicle.

The trailer had likely been white at some point but now resembled a cup of creamed coffee that had been left in the sink for three days and had developed a skin of mold. The windows were no better, fogged over and with mildew in the corners. A few had cracks.

As they walked up to the front door, Raelle said, "He better be here or I'm going to freak." She stayed a few steps behind, hesitant to be approaching the trailer for fear of what they might find.

Just as she said the words, a flash of Toby popped into Sean's head. Like it had been wiped from his mind, he had no memory of Toby being at Crater Lake the previous evening, but suddenly, as he stepped to the door, he was absolutely certain he had seen him walking toward the water. There were no other details, just Toby walking in a sort of trance toward the water, then nothing.

Sean knocked on the door with three hard raps. "Toby! It's Sean and Raelle." Sean could feel there was more to the memory but the rest remained elusive. Either way, he thought it best for Raelle not to go in the trailer.

Sean listened carefully for any movement from within but it remained as still as the outdoors. He again pounded on the door, this time with more vigor. "Toby!"

"I don't like this, Sean." Raelle spoke softly, shaking her head. "Where could he be? It's barely six o'clock." She put her left thumb to her mouth and lightly bit down on the knuckle nearest the nail.

He wanted to tell Raelle about the lake but opted not to. He'd first prefer to make sure Toby wasn't just a heavy sleeper before giving her any reason to lose it.

He put his hand on the doorknob, took in a deep breath, and turned. Part of him hoped the door was locked but it wasn't. He pushed in to find a dimly lit living room. It was a small trailer. Straight ahead, there were two older cloth recliners with a side table between them. The table had an old glass and brass touch lamp and a tv remote. To the right near the door was a newer thirty-inch tv that sat on an old console tv twice as big as the flatscreen.

Sean turned to Raelle. "Just stay here. I'm just going to look around. Holler if anyone comes up."

Raelle nodded and even took a step back.

Sean entered the trailer. He found a light switch on the wall to his right and pressed it up. A fluorescent light in the kitchen flickered and buzzed to life. The glow barely lit the space. Sean couldn't help but note how badly the trailer needed to be cleaned. The linoleum floor had many years' worth of grime, as did the sink, the counters, and the cabinets.

He walked down the hall, peeking in the empty bathroom before stepping into the bedroom. The unmade queen bed had two pillows, zebra print sheets and an old quilt.

Toby was nowhere to be found. Sean thought about taking a deeper look around to see if he could discover any ash rings, but something told him it would be a fruitless search. The imagery of Toby walking toward Crater Lake again popped into his head, and Sean suddenly felt drawn there. As he left, Sean turned off the light.

When he got outside, Raelle was missing. He glanced around in all directions. "Raelle?" She didn't answer.

He ran to his car and was relieved to find her sitting in the passenger seat, fidgeting with her phone.

Sean got in. "Are you okay?"

"I'm not getting any cell service." She said the words so matter of fact and monotone that Sean was certain she was on the verge of giving up.

Sean grabbed his own phone and got the same results. "Damn it!" He returned the phone to his pocket. "By the way, no Toby, no ash rings I could see."

"Doesn't matter."

"Don't say that. Of course it does."

Raelle shook her head, gently, then let her head rest on the seat.

"I think I saw Toby at Crater Lake last night. Maybe he's there." Sean didn't wait for a response. He pressed on the brake, threw the car in reverse, and peeled away from the trailer and out of the park.

They said nothing during the drive. Sean occasionally looked over to Raelle to gauge her mood but her facial expression didn't change one iota. She was lost in thought, shutting down. He wanted her to snap out of it but wasn't sure how to go about doing that. For the time being, he let her be.

Sean pulled the car right up to the water's edge and shut it off. Looking to Raelle, "I'll be right back. I'm going to have a look around. Just stay here. Honk the horn if you see Toby ... or anyone else for that matter."

She didn't respond or acknowledge Sean in any way.

"Fuck, "Sean huffed under his breath. He turned and got out of the car. He made his way along the bank heading south, checking back every minute or so to see if Raelle was ok. After a few minutes, he could no longer see clearly enough inside the car to know for sure she was even there anymore.

Following a worn-down path around the perimeter of the lake, Sean walked in the grass, just outside of the dirt as he looked down for shoe prints. He didn't find much of anything. In fact, he was kind of surprised by the lack of cigarette butts, crumpled soda cans, and even insects. In spite of there being a few trash cans around, people inevitably threw their garbage on the ground, especially on the weekends when the teenagers came down to hang out. That day, the lakeshore was devoid of any evidence of life, past or present.

Sean kept walking, despite the oddity, peeking up occasionally to the eastern skyline where the weather was clear and the sky was morphing to cornflower blue. To look in the other direction only served to upset him. The smoke had picked up speed and would completely engulf Blackwood soon.

Again, looking west, Sean suddenly remembered a property that once existed before *The Great Burn*, a small farm run by an elderly gentleman, around seventy years old, if Sean had to guess. He raised a few horses and couple of cows, and two goats that served to keep the yard from growing over.

During the summer and fall, the farmer had a vegetable stand near the hardware store. Business boomed for him. He was well known in Blackwood and beyond for his organically grown tomatoes, snap green beans, corn, squash, and pumpkins. What Sean most fondly recalled though were the green peppers. The most fragrant and flavorful he had ever eaten, and when Vera used them in her cooking, Sean could think of nothing better.

As he continued to walk, Sean started to find it easy to linger in a few happy moments from before *The Great Burn*. Instead of seeing her terrified face as she cradled Gabe on the ground just before they died, Sean could once again see her smile, the way she walked through any room with unlimited confidence, and the sweet way she spoke to Gabe.

Mindlessly, he walked around the rest of the lake without doing what he had sought to do, instead relishing the all too brief moments of peace he found himself in. As he got close to returning to the car, he found his pace slowing. Reality would come back too soon and his body seemed to unconsciously drag. He didn't care. *Reality,* he thought, *can go fuck itself.*

34

In the car, Raelle sat in silence, despondent. She looked at the lake for a moment then quickly shifted her eyes away. She put her left hand to her throat. She often felt the slight sensation of choking when she got near bodies of water. She closed her eyes and tried to focus on her breathing but all she could see was her mom's face and that helpless stare when the woman realized she was dying. She swallowed hard.

Raelle's mother, Sue, suffered from early on-set Alzheimer's disease, the symptoms first appearing when Sue was just fifty-two years old. They were subtle at first. Losing track of time, forgetting appointments, and where she put the car keys were a few of the many, but within a couple of years, she'd end up at the grocery store with no idea how she got there or why she was there. Even worse, she would wander there on foot. There was no telling where she might end up. That revelation scared the shit out of Raelle. After reporting the event to her mother's doctor, they agreed Sue would best be served by moving in with Raelle.

Afraid to leave the house, Raelle worked only part-time during the two years Sue lived with her. She wanted to be home with her mother one hundred percent of the time but her finances would not allow such an arrangement.

Day after day, Raelle would wake up, take a quick shower and get dressed, then go to Sue's room. On most days, her mother was still in bed, but on some, she'd be pacing around the bed with a worried look on her face.

"Mom? Did you lose something?" Raelle would ask.

"It was here last night?" Sue would answer.

"What, mom? What was here?"

Sue would stop for a moment, look to Raelle as if trying to work out the details of something, then terror would take over her face. Mid-thought, Sue would completely forget what she'd been searching for, and each time it happened, she'd be overcome with emotion and often end up in tears.

There was nothing Raelle could have done to help her mother other than quickly redirect. The mornings were easy. She would suggest getting dressed so they could go to the kitchen for coffee and breakfast. That rarely failed to work. Possibly the best part of the day came when Raelle and Sue sat together at the kitchen table, sipping on coffee and nibbling on hot buttered toast. Raelle cherished those thirty minutes. The rest of the day would often be filled with confusion, anger, fear, and distress for Sue.

Over time, Raelle started to disconnect from her own emotions, and with that came a disconnect from her mother as well. She started to see Sue as a patient, as a thankless job she never wanted but had no choice to attend, and as a burden she longed to be relieved of. She started to hate herself for even having those feelings. And while her experiences were normal for caretakers, she didn't know that.

After nearly two years, when her mother got confused, Raelle inched into the dangerous territory of neglect. When Sue refused to use the bathroom in a timely fashion and Raelle had to clean her up, she got closer. When she went to work and returned to find her mother tearing up her room looking for some long-lost item that probably never really existed at all, Raelle got closer yet.

Twenty-two months, nineteen days, four hours, and thirty-eight minutes after Raelle first took her mother in to take care of her, she arrived home from a four-hour lunch rush shift at The Empty Diner, a job she had started only five weeks earlier.

Raelle entered the house through the front door. Prior to her mother moving in, Raelle parked in the single car garage but could no longer do so because the space was completely packed with all the things brought over from her mother's apartment that she had yet to sort through. She had no time and no desire to do so, although she did miss having the shelter of the garage on days with inclement weather. There was no storm that day other than the cloud that hung over her life.

She dropped her purse on the entry table and casually flipped through the mail. In the early days upon arriving home from work, Raelle would immediately seek out her mother and greet her, check to see how she was doing, offer to make her an afternoon cup of tea or a snack. Those days were long gone. She had become so disengaged from Sue, she barely thought of her as a parent or a family member. When she thought too hard about it, she'd feel a little guilty and do better for a time, but it wouldn't last.

Her day at the restaurant had put Raelle in a bad mood. Nothing seemed to go right. From lunch orders being mixed up, to a dropped glass coffee pot that crashed to the tile floor in spectacular fashion spraying shards and hot coffee behind the counter, to the belligerent business man who could not be satisfied by any manner of service or food preparation.

"These fries are cold. Only three pickles on a tenderloin this big is a joke. This coke tastes flat."

After doing her best to satiate the man, Raelle sent another waitress over to check on the table and give him the check. Raelle had no confidence in that moment in her ability not to throat-chop the man if he had said another snotty thing.

Raelle took the mail to the kitchen and tossed all four envelopes directly in the trash. One credit card offer, two debt consolidation offers, and one offer to switch cell phone companies.

"Why can't, just for once, I get an envelope with a big ass check from the Publisher's Clearing House? That'd be worth opening."

The truth was that her debts were adding up. With what little income she had coming in from the restaurant and Sue's social security check, she was living about five hundred dollars a month in the red and that was all put on credit cards. After almost two years of doing this and a few expensive automotive repairs, even the minimum payment on those cards was making things tight.

She finally had the thought of checking on her mother, who she hoped was asleep in bed so she could just sit and relax for bit before the reality of her caretaker duties set in.

Raelle quietly walked to the hallway where the two bedrooms and the bath were located. When she arrived at her mother's bedroom door, she placed her hand on the doorknob but the smell of fecal matter and urine stopped her in her tracks. She closed her eyes and sighed heavy. She thought seriously about letting go of the knob and sneaking back out of the house. It took every bit of her will power not to.

The nightmare likely waiting on the other side of door would not be the first incident where Raelle found herself dealing with a mess. It didn't happen often, but when it did, it was a two-hour event that drove her to the edge of her sanity, and would end with her drinking and crying herself to sleep afterwards.

Breathing only through her mouth, she opened the door and found her mom standing at the window looking out like she was staring at beautiful sunset. Even the sound of the door opening and Raelle stepping into the room did not alert Sue.

Looking to her mother, Raelle could already see the brown and yellow stains, not only soaked through her light gray pants, but coating them as well. Glancing over to the bed only made matters worse. Thankfully, the comforter had fallen to the floor and out of danger, but the white cotton blanket and the sheets were covered in feces and urine, almost as if Sue had rolled around in it.

"Mom? What are you looking at?" As she asked the questions, Raelle went to the bed and stripped off all the bedding, careful not to get any of it on her hands or anywhere else.

Like nothing had happened, Sue turned to Raelle and said, "I need to go get eggs. I'm out and I can't make a birthday cake for my daughter without eggs."

Raelle stopped.

"You know my daughter, right? Rae."

"It's me, Mom. I'm Rae. I'm going to take these to the laundry and then we need to get you in the bath."

Sue didn't seem to acknowledge Raelle's words. "Well, she's not the pretty one. That's Sandy. Not to say that she's ugly but she was always so plain. Probably why she's never married. Maybe that's my fault. I should have made her put some lipstick on once in a while."

That wasn't the first dig Sue made about Raelle as if she were speaking to a different person. Raelle had become numb to it. People with Alzheimer's tend to say whatever is on their minds with no filter. The behavior was expected, and even though she had learned to blow it off most of the time, occasionally it stung. After a bad day at work and the literal shit show in front of her, Raelle felt her mother's words on that day right down to the bone.

"It's Rae's birthday tomorrow and I'm going to need eggs but I couldn't find the keys to the car."

"Jesus, mom. You're covered in piss and shit and you want to talk about cake." Raelle threw the mass of bedding aside and walked over and grabbed her mother by the arm. "Come on." She pulled her mother toward the door. Sue resisted but that made Raelle pull even harder.

"Let go of me," Sue begged. When they reached the bathroom door, she hollered, "You're hurting me. Let go."

Raelle let go and looked straight into her mother's eyes. "God damn it, Sue! We need to get these clothes off of you and get you in the tub. Now hold still." Her tone made it clear there was no room for discussion or negotiation, and Sue obliged, although, she kept a sour look on her face.

Raelle removed her mother's soiled clothes, drew a bath, and managed to get Sue in without much difficulty. She then took a few moments to put all the bedding and the clothes in the washing machine before making her way back to the bathroom.

She knelt beside the tub and used a soapy washcloth to clean her mom. Once satisfied, Raelle emptied the tub of the filthy water and refilled it with fresh. Sue did not notice her daughter's tear-filled eyes or the sadness in them.

"I really do need those eggs," Sue said. "I mean, if Rae would just settle down with a nice, successful man, I wouldn't need to worry about such things."

Raelle closed her eyes for a moment to let the words flow in and then out of her. She tried hard to remember that her mother was ill and didn't mean to be hurtful but it was hard. Somewhere inside the woman, these thoughts and feelings were real, regardless of her inability to sequester them.

Raelle opened her eyes, full of rage.

"He could have one of those fancy decorated cakes made for her, you know, from one of those bakeries downtown."

Under her breath, Raelle said, "Oh, will you please shut up."

"Honestly," Sue went on, "I think she might be ... a lesbian."

"God damn it, woman! Would you please just shut up!" Without thinking, Raelle reached into the tub and grabbed her mother's right leg and pulled it hard toward the end of the tub, forcing her mother's entire body under the water. With both hands and leaning hard into the tub, Raelle applied just enough force to her mother's chest to prevent her from rising out of the water.

Sue struggled but only for the briefest of moments. From under the water, she looked up to Raelle.

Raelle stared right back and cried. She thought of looking away but instead decided she wanted her mother's final moments to be spent watching her daughter cry. It was cruel and she knew it.

Sue, however, didn't seem to mind. There was no telling what the woman was thinking in those final moments, but her lack of struggle suggested she welcomed the outcome.

Raelle bawled while her mother drowned in that tub.

Sue gasped a few times, her body jerking slightly as the life fell away, her eyes firmly on Raelle's. Like most of the time since her diagnosis, Sue lacked expression, a wandering mind lost in its own ailment.

Raelle fell back onto her bottom. She had stopped crying. She used some toilet paper to wipe her nose and dry her eyes and cheeks.

When Sue's face emerged from beneath the water, Raelle didn't notice. All she could do was sit and be thankful that it was finally over.

Am I evil? I mean, I just killed my mother.

She remained still, focused on her breathing.

She was getting pretty bad. And Jesus, what kind of life did she even have. She couldn't even remember who I was.

Raelle started to think about the logistical issues ahead of her, then her attention turned right back to the act.

Oh fuck. I just killed my mother. I just killed my mother!

A plan came together rather quickly. She'd go to the backyard with a bottle of gin, drinking some of it before leaving the bottle on the table next to the teak rocker on the back porch. Then, with her phone in hand, she'd return to the bathroom and make the call to 9-1-1. The story was simple. She set her mother up with a bath and then stepped outside for a drink. After a long day at work, she dozed off, and when she awoke and returned to the bathroom, her mother was face down in the tub.

They'd either buy it or they wouldn't. In one scenario, she'd be free. In the other, she'd go to jail for killing her mother. At that point, she didn't really care.

Luckily for her, there wasn't the least bit of suspicion. Bad accidents seemed to be such a common occurrence amongst those with Alzheimer's disease, the EMTs, the coroner, not one person blinked twice at her false recollection of events.

35

Raelle sat quietly in Sean's car, feeling as detached from her own reality and life as she once did from her mother and her illness. Sue's death was nearly seven years before *The Great Burn* and it haunted her still, but with everything that had evolved in recent days, Raelle felt her spirit checking out.

Sean returned, got in, and slumped into his seat, disappointed in his lack of any meaningful discoveries, even more so that he was back from his all too brief respite. To his eyes, Raelle was no better off than when he left, not that he expected different.

"No sign of Toby. Say, do you remember that old farmer, had a place about a mile that way?" Sean pointed out of the windshield. "He had that little stand he'd set up downtown near the hardware store. Best, most flavorful green peppers you could get."

Raelle did not answer and gave no acknowledgement of his presence.

Sean continued, assuming she could hear him.

"Yeah, Vera made a red sauce using those green peppers one time, I think for a lasagna. I just remember us raving about them for weeks." He sighed. "I miss my wife." Sean was not one to open up about his feelings, least of all to someone he only knew in passing, but he thought maybe getting it off his chest might help Raelle snap out of her funk too.

"She was a great cook. Admittedly, we ate out a lot, but she had a flare for Italian and Mediterranean foods. I always told her she could have been a pro chef if she ever wanted to. Of course, she was also a wiz with numbers, which I suppose is what drove her accounting.

"Anyway, with all this shit going on, and especially in the last year, I always try to remember those kinds of things about her. The good times, ya know." He paused to gather his thoughts and see if Raelle had any response. She didn't. "But fuck, the things that pop into my head tend to be bad. Why is that?"

Raelle remained in a near catatonic state, her eyes fixed to somewhere beyond the side window.

"Well, I guess all we can do is go back into town."

Sean started the car, did a three-point turnaround, and began the drive back to The Empty Diner.

As they got closer, the smoky clouds had made their way to town and were now covering most of the area. A gentle falling of ash began hitting the car and the windshield as they drove. Sean set the windshield wipers to low and used the fluid to get an initial clean.

Along the way, Raelle continued to stare out of the window. She wasn't looking at anything in particular. She had just become lost in her own thoughts. The trees and buildings and road signs whizzed by. As they passed one large tree, a shadow appeared from behind it that brought Raelle right out of her state. She followed the figure with her eyes but it passed too quickly for her to get a clear idea of who or what she saw. She said nothing to Sean.

A minute later as they approached the turn that would take them to the street the diner was on, the figure in black once again appeared, this time from behind a truck parked on the side of the road. The man emerged more like a mist than a solid mass, and before Raelle could even react, the figure disappeared as they passed.

Raelle put her hands to her mouth, her sudden movement catching Sean's attention.

"You okay?" he asked, worried, but also glad she was moving again.

"I need to get out."

"Okay." Sean wondered if she might get sick, so he pulled over immediately, about half a block from where he intended to turn left. He threw the car into park and turned to Raelle. "What's the matter?"

"I need to go home," Raelle said, but she didn't mean it, and she made no mention of what she saw on the side of the road. Oddly enough, the presence did not scare her. Instead, a kind of peace passed over her as she opened the car door and exited.

"Wait," Sean said as leaned over to get a look at her.

"It's okay, Sean. I just need to go home." There was no fear in her voice, no doubt, and no room for discussion.

He tried anyway. "You really shouldn't be alone," Sean started but was interrupted by the door slamming shut. He sat and watched her walk away but couldn't think of any compelling excuse that would likely change her mind. After a few minutes, she disappeared around the corner and out of sight.

36

Every morning after breakfast at the facility, the nursing assistants would make their rounds with the residents for bathing time. Randy Spokes was assigned room 45, among others.

Randy rolled his cart into the room, right up to the end of the bed fully stocked with cleaning clothes, towels, and two pink plastics tubs – one with warm soapy water for washing, the other with warm water for rinsing. This was always one of the best parts of Randy's shift. The halls and the rooms were quiet at that time of day. The only sound that escaped each room tended to be from TVs, but other than that, there wasn't much other noise or activity.

"Alright, buddy. Time for a bath." Randy carefully pulled up the lower half of the blankets that covered the man. Using the hot soapy water and a washcloth, Randy gently performed his duties. He always took a moment to study the burn scars on the man's legs. Everything had healed in a long, excruciating process, but ninety percent of the his body would forever hold the evidence of his ordeal. Randy wondered what the man's life would be like if he weren't in a coma. *Yeah, he's alive,* he thought. *But how much of a life would it be? That's tough.*

Randy did like to speak to the man as he worked. He believed people in comas could hear their surroundings, and that it was good for them to hear normal human voices having normal conversations. While there would be no back and forth between Randy and the man, he was certain the net benefit existed.

"Ya know, buddy boy, I don't know about you, but I seriously need to go on a date. Not sure if you had a lady friend before all this, but it's been a while for me." Randy continued his work as he spoke, using the soapy bin to wash, then a new washcloth and the clean water to rinse.

"Well, there's this nurse that works here. You've probably met her," Randy paused and put up finger quotes. "As much as you are capable of meeting someone. Nurse Cindy. She has this gorgeous, long, carrot red hair. Whenever we pass each other in the hallway, she smiles. Maybe she's just being nice, but I don't see her smile so easily at anyone else. Just me.

"So, what do you think? Should I ask her out?"

Randy finished washing and rinsing the lower part of the man's body then moved on to the upper. When he pulled the blankets down, he once again stopped to admire the scars, especially the biggest and deepest one that ran across the chest. The man no longer had nipples, just a deep chasm of ridged flesh where the breast tissue and nipples once were. It almost took his breath away each time. As a nursing assistant, Randy had seen a lot, but nothing compared to the deformed skin and muscle of the resident in room 45.

Randy started with the man's head then made his way to the shoulders and chest. With a heavily soaped washcloth, he washed the chest with small circular motions. Switching to a clean cloth from the rinse water, repeating his motions to get the soap up.

Out of the blue, the man's throat muscles started to flex, forcing his mouth open. A soft gurgling noise escaped.

With a washcloth under it, Randy held his hand to the center of the man's chest. The muscles twitched there too. Randy quickly pulled the washcloth away and tossed it into the rinse tub. He pushed the bathing cart away from the bed and ran around to the other side and pushed the CALL button.

Back at the bedside, he witnessed the man's deformed mouth pulse open and closed.

"Oh shit! What are you choking on?" Just as he said the words, two nurses ran into the room going straight to the bedside. Randy stepped back to make room.

"What happened?" the younger, black male nurse with short curly hair asked.

"No idea, Kal." Randy replied.

"He's running out of air," the other nurse said, a woman in her mid-forties with blonde hair always kept up in a ponytail while she worked. She had been at the company since graduating nursing school at age twenty-two.

"He's turning purple, Michelle. Is he choking on something?"

The monitor next to the bed started beeping as the man's oxygen levels dropped.

"Any chance he swallowed something?" Michelle asked of Randy.

"No way. I was just bathing him and he suddenly starting gasping."

"Let's roll him on his side and try to force out whatever's in there," Michelle said.

They did as she instructed.

Kal immediately started slapping the man's back. After five hard hits, a small amount of soapy water trickled out of the man's mouth followed by a huge blast of liquid, soaking part of the bed and spraying out onto the floor.

"What in the hell was that all about?" Kal asked.

Randy quickly grabbed a towel from his cart, and confused and nervous, started cleaning up the fluid from the man's face before moving to the floor.

Michelle stood there lightly shaking her head and staring at Randy and the soapy water as she attempted to reconcile what had just happened. She tried hard not to assume some sort of neglect had just occurred, but she could think of no reasonable explanation for what she had just witnessed.

After frantically soaking up the water, Randy stood up and saw the look on Kal and Michelle's faces, and was instantly on the defense. Shaking his head, "I don't know what to say, but I didn't do this." The words got caught in his throat. "I swear on my mother's grave."

"It's not that I don't believe you, Randy," Michelle said, "but I can't explain what we just saw. We need to talk to the charge Nurse. Finish cleaning up the mess and come to the nurse's station when you're done."

Kal and Michelle rolled the comatose man onto his back, checked the monitors, and once satisfied with their return to normal, left the room.

In the hallway, Michelle stopped Kal.

"Maybe you should stay behind, just in case."

Kal thought about it for a second, then nodded. "Okay." He stood near the door, clearly in view of Randy and the resident.

Michelle walked away, hoping the entire incident had a simple explanation that had yet to reveal itself.

37

Raelle left the company of Sean and walked straight to the diner. She understood she was being followed and simply didn't care.

She entered the diner, leaving the door unlocked and the lights off and made her way behind the counter. The morning had been a long one, full of emotion and regrets. What she really wanted at that moment was a tall glass of iced tea and maybe something to eat. She thought of how people on death row get a last meal of their choosing, so she started to think about what she would want her last meal to be. Nothing stood out in her mind. After filling a red cup with ice and pouring the tea, she caught sight of the pie cooler and the lone uncut cherry topped cheesecake displayed on the top shelf. She didn't often have it for fear of what it might do to her ass and hips, but it was her favorite dessert and as good a food item as she could think of for a last meal.

She removed the cheesecake from the display case, placed it on the counter at the middle seat along with her tea and a fork, and walked around to the other side. She didn't bother cutting a piece out, instead choosing to dive right in to the whole thing. She knew she wasn't going to eat it all but she also knew it didn't matter. In a few minutes, she'd be gone, and with her, all the fear, the anxiety, the guilt, and floating through a meaningless existence where the days were all the same.

The first bite was pure bliss. She closed her eyes and left it on her tongue for five full seconds before she chewed it softly and swallowed. Each subsequent bite was done the same way until she had her fill.

As she ate, Raelle thought about her mom, but not of the final years. She loved her mom and had a great relationship with her. They were best friends until she got sick and she gladly cared for her until the burden grew to be too much for her handle on her own. It was only after the disease took hold that Raelle discovered her mother's true feelings about how Raelle lived her life and the choices she made. Their relationship felt like a fraud after that. Without knowing firsthand, Raelle imagined how many parents must feel disappointed when their children don't turn out to be better realized copies of themselves. That idea didn't bring much comfort, although, it did provide some perspective.

She would always remember with fondness the time her mother bought them tickets for a cruise that traveled the Gulf of Mexico. Raelle had never been on a cruise and rarely traveled as money was too tight to ever splurge on such things.

On the flight from Albuquerque to New Orleans, they met an older retired couple that shared stories of their globetrotting adventures, which helped pass the time.

Looking back, Raelle remembered laying poolside on the cruise and getting a little burnt, and walking around Puerto Vallarta on the coast of Eastern Mexico, one of the stops they made as the cruise sailed. They drank and ate amazing food and laughed more than they had in a long time, but it was also the first time Raelle could recall that her mother exhibited some early warning signs of the disease about to take hold.

They were so insignificant, Raelle paid them no mind. *Everyone forgets their cell phone or their purse or their keys from time to time,* she thought, but thinking back to the cruise, there were nine such incidents on one seven-day vacation, and that should have been a red flag.

She hated that her once pleasant memory had turned sour, so she tried to think of anything else to get her mind off of it, but the what-ifs took hold. *What if she had gotten treatment sooner? What if she had never deteriorated so quickly? What if I never had a reason to drown my own mother?*

Out of nowhere and pulling her from the negative train of thought she had jumped on, Raelle got the impression she was not alone in the restaurant, and worse yet, the presence seemed to be right behind her. How the person arrived there was unknown to her, especially considering the bell above the door didn't ring, but to her it didn't matter.

Raelle pushed away the cheesecake and took a sip of her iced tea. "I don't suppose you'd let me finish my drink?" she asked, not really expecting an answer. "I mean, what's the rush at this point?"

She sighed, closed her eyes. When she reopened them, she turned around to face her reaper. She couldn't help but notice it had grown quite dark outside and the ash was falling like snow and had left a dusting.

The man in black stood halfway between Raelle and the front door, an ominous and foreboding sight to behold, however, she was not afraid. Raelle had accepted her role in the little game and had made her peace with the decisions of her past.

Although the stranger's face was obscured in darkness, Raelle did her best to look him straight in the eyes. "You might as well get it over with. I'm not scared of you. I'll have you know that I killed my own mother. Drowned her the bathtub." She sighed heavy. "Wow. That's the first time I've ever said that out loud." She smiled. "Don't get me wrong, I'm not happy about it. Far from it. I've tortured myself every day with that selfish act. It just feels good to publicly admit it. So, go ahead. I probably don't deserve to be here anymore."

As she stood there, her chest started to feel heavy. A tightness had formed. She put her hand to her throat as the air left and she couldn't seem to catch her breath. Once again, like had happened earlier in the car and after the first appearance of the stranger outside the diner, she experienced the sensation of drowning. She closed her eyes but quickly opened them back up. In that millisecond, the man in black moved from his original spot to just two feet in front of her. She could clearly see his eyes, and in them, truth.

She closed her eyes again and spoke only in her mind that she was ready. Somehow, she knew he could hear her thoughts.

And he did.

With no pain, no fear, Raelle's mind was transported to the place and time just minutes before *The Great Burn*, where she once again experienced the groundburst outside The Empty Diner and the encroaching fire as she went for cover inside the restaurant.

Her body disappeared, as did the stranger's, a small ash ring left behind on the floor and a partially eaten cheesecake the only evidence she had been there.

38

A blur of images appeared to the comatose man. There were three men, all phasing in and out before him. He didn't recognize any of them, except perhaps, the one in the long black coat and wide-brimmed hat. He had never seen him before but there existed an odd familiarity, something more akin to a feeling.

And he was hot, and it was getting hotter. The smell of burning wood and rubber filled his nostrils. He couldn't actually feel whether or not his physical body was dripping with sweat but he imagined he had soaked through whatever clothing he had on.

He held a general sense of confusion and frustration as the men before him appeared and disappeared. Eventually, the men stopped showing up. Instead, a strange woman and a young child came into focus. He had no idea who they were, but he experienced a deep sense of longing, love, and regret upon seeing them. If he could have cried, he would have. Soon, they disappeared too.

The resident returned to the dark and empty spaces he existed in but was left with the distinct impression he was nearing the end of a journey. He had dozens of questions but no answers. Being a prisoner in his own body and mind, he had no choice but to accept this reality. He had grown weary over the last few days and began longing for an end to his astral engagements.

39

Sean pulled away from the curb and drove down to Main Street where he turned left. He kept going, toward downtown, stopping in the middle of the street at the diner. The restaurant was dark. *Maybe she went in,* he thought. *Then again, she said she wanted to go home, and I have no idea where she lives.*

With growing frustration, he continued up the road until he got to the town square, which at that time of day usually had some activity. That day, it was utterly abandoned.

"It's a god damn ghost town."

Noticing the ash had gotten much worse, he put the car in park and got out to have look around. His hair was quickly peppered with the ash. The sidewalks were completely covered and so were the streets, the park benches, and the trees and bushes. Looking back down the road he had just come from, he thought it odd that his own tire marks were the only disturbances in the ash. There were no signs of other vehicles, pedestrians, nothing.

Noting the air quality, he suddenly realized how bad it might be to breathe in that environment, so he returned to his car.

Scared and beginning to feel a strong sense of hopelessness, Sean let his head fall back to the headrest and he closed his eyes for a moment to gather himself. A million questions ran through his mind. To comfort himself, he thought of Vera and Gabe.

Images of their faces floated in and out, times when they were smiling, when they cried, when they laughed, and when they were mad. To him, it didn't matter. Sean understood life and love really boiled down to those simple moments. A person rarely thinks of them until they truly need to. And in that moment, Sean did.

"I'm so sorry, Vera. I should never have brought you and our son here." He opened his eyes and ran his hands through his hair from front to back and sighed. He wanted to cry as his lip quivered but he held back.

"Oh god, I really fucked up. Wherever you are, I hope you don't hate me. I dream of you and Gabe all the time. Mostly terrible dreams but sometimes not. I just wish I could turn back the clock and get a do-over. But hell, I know you. You'd have forgiven me straightaway despite the fact you never wanted to come here. That was your nature. The problem is, I just can't seem to forgive myself."

In his mind, he could hear her voice in a loving tone say, "It's time to come home, Sean. It's time to come home."

Sean lowered his head and burst into tears. All the pent-up emotions from years of distress with his wife finally flowing out. With a hand to his forehead, he cried until his head hurt.

When he finally calmed down enough to open his eyes, he somehow felt a presence. Compelled to, he looked to his left and found Agent Learza's car sitting right next to this own, facing the opposite direction.

Sean wiped his face with the back of his hand and rolled his window down.

Agent Learza followed suit and waved Sean over. "Hop in," he said.

Sean turned off his car and put the keys in his pocket, then walked around to the passenger's side of Agent Learza's vehicle and got in the front seat.

There was instant comfort in being next to Agent Learza. Sean wasn't sure if it was because Learza was law enforcement or if it was just being in the presence of another human being that wasn't from Blackwood. Either way, he didn't question the calm it brought.

"Hello, Dr. Atwater."

"It's been a crazy couple of days."

"I bet."

That response seemed odd to Sean, as if Agent Learza knew about all the craziness they had been through.

"How do you mean?" Sean asked.

"Well, I mean, with all the missing people and the phones being down and now this smoky and ashy atmosphere. I'm not surprised it's been a rough go."

"The phones are down? Is there a wildfire nearby?" A look of concern drew across Sean's face.

"There's a lot more going on than you know."

"Oh? Like what?"

"Well, it'd be easier just to show you. Let me take you home."

"I don't really think I should go home. Everyone in this town seems to have disappeared and I was just with Raelle and she started acting funny and took off. We need to find her."

Agent Learza drove the car away, headed in the direction of Sean's house. The windshield wipers were working hard to keep the ash out of the line of sight. The sky had become dark enough that headlights were necessary to see the road well enough to drive. The agent seemed to have no trouble navigating through town.

"I can assure you, Raelle is fine, all of them are fine."

"So, you've seen them? Was there an evacuation or something? What the hell happened?" Sean spoke quickly as he grew desperate for answers.

"Slow down there, bud. Everything will be explained soon enough. We just need to get you home first."

In a much shorter time than Sean believed it normally took to get to his house, they arrived.

"I have to take care of something real quick, but go ahead and go in," Agent Learza said. "I will join you in a minute."

Still skeptical, Sean left the vehicle and jogged to the front door, brushing the ash from his hair when he arrived. He looked back to Agent Learza who seemed to be busy taking notes in a large book. Still full of questions but exhausted, Sean entered his home, closing the door behind him.

He walked to the entrance of the kitchen but stopped there, turning around at the sound of the front door flying open. The man in black stood just inside the house. The door automatically slammed shut behind him.

Sean remained still. That was his first face to face encounter with the stranger everyone else had spoken about, and now with the man right in front of him, he finally understood the mystique.

The stranger hovered in place, saying nothing.

Sean could feel his heart race but he wasn't scared. Some part of him was elated. Standing before the man that seemingly brought all this recent trouble to Blackwood might mean finally getting an explanation for what had happened over the last two days. At least he hoped so.

The stranger's face was barely visible in the shadow of his black brimmed hat, and yet, somehow, there was a familiarity about him.

"Who are you?"

"You know who I am." The voice was menacing and ethereal but not in a way that made Sean fearful. It too, like his face, seemed oddly familiar.

"I really don't know and I think the time for riddles is over. Just be straight with me. It's been a rough couple of days. Hell, it's been a rough couple of years for that matter, and I'm tired."

"I am both the keeper of records and the reaper of souls. I am known by many cultures, over many religions, associated with many folktales. They are mostly all myths but each hold kernels of truth. They are all me, and yet none. I have gone by many names. Sammael, Azazel, Gabriel, Michael, The Angel of Death, The Grim Reaper, but I refer to myself as Azrael."

Azrael, Sean thought. *Azrael?*

Sean knew of the name from culture, history, and religion, but there was something else about it that rang familiar to him.

The moniker Angel of Death stood out too.

Sean almost chuckled but kept it inside. Agent Angel Learza. It was almost too clever. Learza. Azrael. Angel Learza. The Angel Azrael. Sean began to feel a bit stupid for not seeing it before. Then again, until that moment, he had no reason to see a connection in the name.

"Even in that ridiculous getup, I thought you reminded me of Agent Learza, or should I say, the Angel Azrael."

"Indeed," the man said, but his voice had morphed into something that sounded a little more like Agent Learza's voice.

"You know, I don't really consider myself a man of faith." Sean's posture relaxed some. Somewhere inside, he knew the man spoke only the truth, and Sean took solace in that. "So, what, do you judge my life and decide where I end up going?" Sean quickly pointed up and then down.

"Your decisions and choices on Earth have no effect on where you end up, only how long it takes you to get there."

Sean nodded. He suddenly understood what that meant for himself. He'd soon join Vera and Gabe, and once again, be happy.

As a doctor and a natural skeptic, he still couldn't help but wonder. "Is any of this real? I mean, this town, *The Great Burn*, all this crap?"

"It's real to you, and that is all that matters. I come to you now as a bridge. I have arrived to lead your souls away. That is not always an easy process. Each of you must go through an awakening of sorts, a reconciliation. Occasionally, I must come forth and gently nudge you in the right direction.

"Humans are famously attached to their failings in life. You wear them like a suit of armor. They protect you but they also weigh you down. And when you die, they are often too heavy to shed."

Sean felt the sting of those words close to his heart. He had been experiencing that exact thing, and while he already knew it, hearing Azrael say it was a revolution to his psyche.

"You see, when a human dies they are usually sent home. Sometimes, however, that transition is not instantaneous. Like in your case, your soul needed time to release your guilt and find the truth in your heart that Vera and Gabe's deaths were not your fault. Life and time flow like the storm clouds that travel the planet, and you have no more power to change the currents of your life as you do those clouds. There are forces bigger than you that you have no control over. What determines your experience is how you react to them. Peace comes when you make that realization. So be kind to yourself in this moment. Relax your mind. Forgive yourself and you shall be with them again.

Sean pondered the words. His naturally cynical mind fought a little but the truth of Agent Learza's words could not be denied. A small part of him let go of the guilt.

"So, you're here to take my life?"

"Heavens no. I chronicle the arrivals and the departures, as has been my task since nearly the beginning of mankind's existence. I do not take lives or give them, I simple record them and help usher the soul to its next destination."

"Well, I don't seem to be dead yet, so what happens now?"

"Dr. Atwater, that is what I am here to show you."

The man in black slowly opened his coat and revealed a seemingly endless pit of black with a tiny flame in the center.

Sean was powerless to look away, and as he stared into that black abyss, the flame grew brighter and brighter until it blinded him.

40

When Sean could once again open his eyes, everything had changed. Azrael had vanished, and Sean was now standing naked in the shower. Light poured in through the bathroom window as if the ash clouds had suddenly and completely disappeared. Even the smell had changed.

He remembered everything about the morning of *The Great Burn* so clearly. As he looked around the bathroom, it was clear he was set to experience it once again.

Sean exited the shower, dried off, and dressed for work. He chose navy blue slacks, brown dress shoes, and a powder blue, long sleeved button up shirt with no tie. He'd wait to brush his teeth until he polished off another cup of coffee and maybe had some oatmeal topped with fresh blueberries.

Upon entering the kitchen, Sean heard giggling and the wooden front screen door slam shut. Gabe had no doubt run out into the yard with Vera not far behind. Her worry for the child running out into the street never ceased despite the fact they lived just outside of town on a gravel road, a place where weeks would go by without another vehicle aside from their own kicking up rocks. Vera never lost her New York City sensibilities when they moved to Blackwood, even after they chose a rundown old farmhouse to renovate, even when she nearly cried after discovering there wasn't a Starbucks within one hundred miles. For Vera, it was a different kind of transition. She was NYC born and raised. Sean, on the other hand, had one foot in both worlds, although, it never felt that way during his time in the big city. When they lived in New York, the big city doctor became his persona, and he rarely thought of his hometown and the young man he left behind.

Sean poured his second cup of coffee into his #1 Dad mug, one he used often but secretly hated. The rim was too thick for his liking, and if he wasn't careful, coffee would trickle past his lips and down his chin. The paper cup that came from his stop at the diner each morning would be welcome relief from the inherent risk of a coffee stain on his delicate work shirts.

As he sipped, an uneasy feeling pulsated through his body. Looking to his cup, ripples formed on the surface of the liquid which he couldn't explain.

From nowhere, the house shook and rattled coinciding with what sounded like a passenger plane flying dangerously low overhead. The front screen door flew open and then slammed shut. Suddenly, the house actually appeared to tilt hard in one direction before thrusting itself back a few moments later to its original place. A few windows shattered and the wood framing of the house, windows, and doors creaked from stress. In the process, Sean nearly lost his balance, barely able to keep the coffee cup from spilling and flying from his hand.

"The fuck was that?" Sean blurted out. "Vera?" he yelled. Walking to the living room, he called out again for his wife. When she didn't answer, he called out a third time, shouting.

"Vera! Gabe!"

Just as the words left his mouth, the meteor impact occurred a few miles away, unbeknownst to him. He did feel the violent shake that happened right after. He maintained his balance during the rumble, but this time, he could not control the cup in his hand, letting it loose to fly across the room and shatter on the wall next to the TV. The coffee left a trail on the floor and a large brown splotch on the wall.

Sean took a moment to ponder the fate of the cup but then remembered he hated it anyway, so he turned his attention to the front door. Halfway there, he could see Vera and Gabe in the yard through the film of the busted screen. They were both on the ground, Vera struggling to get up as she covered Gabe's head and torso area. Blood streamed from her right temple and onto her white blouse.

Just as Sean reached the door, he locked eyes with his wife and could see the fear in her eyes, a fear he had never seen in her before, the kind that came when a person knew they were about to die, and as a doctor, he recognized from his work.

In that moment, all Sean could think about was the fight they had the night before, one he could feel in his heart had formed a path that would lead to divorce.

On the horizon, a rolling storm of dust, debris, and fire grew ever larger, and in a matter of seconds, reached their property. Sean remembered feeling the concussive power of the blast but not much else.

41

Room 45 was quiet after the morning rounds. The monitor beeped in all the normal ways, and nothing at all was out of the ordinary until a shadow appeared in the corner of the room.

Despite being in a coma, the resident in Room 45 felt the presence of the stranger, a presence he had sensed before but not from inside the room. On many of his recent mental projections to his hometown, the comatose man bared witness to the man in black as he stalked the people of Blackwood, and eventually, saw the stranger take each person one by one from their tortured existences.

But there was one final piece of the puzzle left to place, and that involved the sole survivor of the event known as *The Great Burn*. The stranger had come for him, and in doing so, would complete another entry in his book.

In his mind, the man could hear the stranger speak.

"You have made a great sacrifice and now the time has come for you move on as well. You have seen the others. You have watched them spend months and months trapped in their pain, their guilt, their doubt. But now, you get to join them and find some peace of your own."

The man in black disappeared from the corner and appeared instantly at the bedside of the man, placing a hand on his scarred left arm.

The man suddenly awoke from his coma, and for the first time, he saw the room he had been in for many months. He turned his head slightly so he could see the stranger.

From behind the stranger, someone attempted to open the door to the room but could not. It was not locked, but nonetheless, it wouldn't budge. The stranger made sure they could not be disturbed.

The nurse tried multiple times, even slamming his shoulder into the door but could not get it to open. He could be heard cursing. He left the area seeking assistance.

The stranger paid it no mind.

Speaking aloud, the stranger said, "I am Azrael. I possess The Book of Life and am here to bring you home."

A tiny stream of tears escaped the corner of the man's left eye but he was not afraid. The tears were of pure joy. He was, in fact, thankful, as he understood the wait for his departure was finally about to end.

"To help you understand, let me tell you a story that will ease your transition and explain your part in all this."

Azrael opened his book to the very first entry and read verbatim from its pages.

The Story of Life and Death
(origins unknown)
PART I

And so ... time began. To populate the Earth, angels were sent to gather dust that would be used for the creation of mankind. The angel who succeeded was given The Book of Life to chronicle all the souls that would occupy the earthly domain.

And so ... from that day forward, the arrival and departure of each soul would be recorded. A simple task. As time went on, the book became a permanent record of mankind.

And so ... an era went by. Upon inspection, the angels began to notice that some of the souls had not returned home. There was a system for humans. They were born and they die. Their lives were meant to be finite so they would know how precious a gift life was. Yet, an anomaly was occurring.

PART II

And so ... the angels wondered why some souls came back to heaven and others did not. In that time, there was no place else for them to go, yet not everyone had arrived back home that had been born on Earth, staying well beyond a normal human lifespan.

And so ... an angel was sent to discover the truth of this mystery and soon found that some humans remained on Earth as dream-shades or ghost-like entities. Their unfinished business tethered them as such, caught in a desolate landscape as wandering lost souls, trying to cling to the lives they once lived. Eventually, the *missionary angel found hope for the dream-shades in their self-created darkness: a way to free those that were trapped.*

And so ... from that day forward, the work began that would bring all of mankind home.

PART III

And so ... the angels presented two goats: one given to God and one to the angel in charge of the Book of Life. This angel would cast the goat into the wilderness with all the sins and mistakes of mankind on its back so they may be cleansed.

And so ... the angel was then sent down to Earth to awaken the dream-shades and guide them from their self-created purgatory. The task was not always easy, as the emotions and life bond of mankind are strong and nearly everlasting.

And so ... with forgiveness and love, the angel reminded them they are inherently fallible and worthy of peace. Because more than anything, after all, mankind held a deep yearning to return home.

And so ... with a little guidance, they always do.

With the story concluded, Azrael moved his hand to the farmer's chest, and when he did, the farmer could feel the life leaving his body. In heaven, he could finally find the peace he had longed for. For the farmer, that year since *The Great Burn* felt more like ten, so his sacrifice was the greatest of all. Finally, he could go home.

Azrael flipped to another page much deeper in the book and marked the occasion of the farmer's release, just like he always did, and upon closing the book, Azrael disappeared, leaving behind the earthly remains of the farmer and the long, solid tone of the heart monitor.

Epilogue

Years later

On their way to Roswell, New Mexico for a long weekend getaway, the Russell Family of El Paso, Texas, which consisted of father Damien, mother Joy, eleven-year-old daughter Kelani, and nine-year-old son Damien Jr, drove the two-lane highway toward their destination. Along the way, Damien secretly intended to make a slight diversion to take a look at a creepy ghost town he remembered reading about many years prior. The rest of the family was oblivious to his plans.

"Hey Dad," Damien Jr said, breaking the silence of the drive, "I was reading that the government has actual dead alien bodies in a freezer. Is that true?"

Kelani rolled her eyes at the mere suggestion. She had headphones on but kept one side slightly off so she could hear conversations. "You're dumb."

"Don't call your brother dumb. And to answer your question, Damien, I don't know and I don't think anyone really does. And even though there have been a lot of declassified documents and such released over the last decade, the government has been known to suppress a lot of the information about aliens and UFOs in the name of national security, so I think anything is possible."

"But even if they did," Joy chimed in, "they wouldn't be in Roswell."

"Can we go to Area 51 then?" Damien Jr asked.

"Not this trip bud," Damien replied. "That's in Nevada. Plus, they don't let people into Area 51. It's a highly secure military installation. But I do have a surprise pit stop to make that might pique your interest."

Joy gave Damien a confused look.

He could sense her stare but didn't reciprocate, instead, he smiled and kept driving without saying anything. He had already taken the alternate road that would lead them to Blackwood. None of them had even noticed and they were just a few minutes out.

"So, Dad, what is it?" Damien Jr asked.

"You'll see."

"Are there going to be aliens there?"

"No son."

"Come on, dad," Damien Jr begged.

The car grew closer to a large sign on the side of the road, and when Damien reached it, he pulled the car over so his family could get a better look.

"Where are we?" Joy asked.

"Just look at the sign."

And they all did.

The sign on the side of the road as one entered from the east read: Blackwood, Population 1665. The 1 had been covered by a black X and the five had been graffitied with white spray paint and replaced with a 6, malformed and dripping. Beneath that, also in white spray paint, were the words: Welcome to Hell. The front of the sign had otherwise remained unchanged for years. It was weathered, the paint peeling, and was slightly askew from the blast of hot wind that nearly blew it over during a natural disaster. The wood of the back of the sign, however, was charcoaled and soot covered, although not as thick as it once was considering the amount of time that had passed.

"Creepy," Kelani said. "Blackwood? Is this some kind of scary theme park or something?"

"Not exactly," Damien answered, "This place is real."

"What do you mean by real?" Joy asked.

"Real, as in, this was a real town years ago until a meteor crashed nearby and wiped the whole town out in a matter of minutes. The giant hole left by the meteor is now a place called Crater Lake. You can't swim there or anything. The entire town is completely blocked off, although there's not much left anyway."

"Whoa." Damien Jr said.

"I think I remember reading about that," Joy said. "Yeah, it sounds familiar."

"When you say the town was wiped out, what you do mean? Did all the people die?" Kelani asked.

"Yes, Kee. Nearly every building in town was either blown down or burned to the ground. And every single person, save for one, died that day. They say the town is haunted. And if you get close enough, you can still smell the wood burning."

"Good gawd, that's terrible," Joy said.

"What happened to the one person who didn't die?" Damien Jr asked.

"Well, it was an old farmer that supposedly caught fire when the blast hit but he fell down the stairs of his outdoor emergency shelter and somehow survived but with terrible burns over most of his body. Unfortunately, he was in a coma and did eventually die about a year later."

A few minutes went by as they sat in silence processing the story Damien had just told.

"Well, that was a wonderfully creepy excursion, but let's get outta here," Joy said. "My skin is starting to crawl."

"Agreed," Kelani added.

"Can't we go see the crater lake?" Damien Jr asked.

"Nope. Like I said, it's all blocked off. But I'm going to take a few pictures of this sign before we go." And he did.

Afterwards, they continued to their intended destination, a few of the many curious people that stopped by to see the spine-tingling, charred sign on the side of the road that served as a timeless reminder of *The Great Burn* and the lives lost on an August day so many years ago.

ABOUT THE AUTHOR

Richard A. Powell II currently lives with his wife Amy and their Cavachon Padraig in Arizona, where he enjoys great independent and sci-fi films, crime documentaries, emerging technology, playing video games, reading and writing (obviously), and traveling.

He operates mostly on double cheeseburgers and coffee, and ever since moving to Arizona, he has a hard time not wearing shorts and flip-flops at all times.

www.richardapowellii.com

richard.powell74@gmail.com